THUNDER

by

DRUSILLA LEATHER

CHIMERA

Thunder's Slaves published by
Chimera Publishing Ltd
PO Box 152
Waterlooville
Hants
PO8 9FS

Printed and bound in Great Britain by
Cox & Wyman Ltd, Reading.

THUNDER'S SLAVES

Drusilla Leather

This novel is fiction – in real life practice safe sex

For G and Z, fellow passengers in the Taxi of Shame...

Chapter One

Max Cavendish glanced away from the dinner table and suppressed a yawn. Twenty-seven years of having a younger brother, and he had still not learned that when Jonathan wanted to see him, there was inevitably a hidden agenda. Admittedly, having his brother to dinner did give Max a more than welcome chance to play lord of the manor; the seventeenth-century Suffolk farmhouse he had purchased had been a bargain purely because of the extensive renovation work it had needed, but he had put in the necessary time and investment willingly, and now, eighteen months after he had first moved in, the house was perfect. He had enjoyed showing off the antique four-poster bed in the master bedroom, the lovingly restored farmhouse kitchen, still with its original beams and inglenook fireplace, and the newly-built heated indoor swimming pool and Jacuzzi. He had, however, kept Jonathan well away from his lavishly appointed playroom; there were some secrets he thought it safer to keep from his strait-laced sibling.

After the guided tour had come dinner, and that was when the real reason for his brother's visit had become apparent. He was planning another of his crazy expeditions. Jonathan, despite his youth, was senior lecturer in archaeology at St Susan's College, Oxford, and he spent the long summer vacations searching the most remote corners of the world for lost treasures. Last year, he had journeyed into the heart of the Amazon basin, but instead of the hoped-for haul of Mayan artefacts, he had returned with nothing more than a broken leg, having fallen into a ravine. The fact that he might have died of heatstroke and dehydration if he had not been found in time and airlifted to safety had done nothing to dampen Jonathan's passion for adventure. This year's jaunt was already planned, but this time he was not content simply to risk his own neck and reputation. He wanted something from Max, that something being a book commission.

Cavendish Editions had grown from humble beginnings over the last decade to become one of the country's most respected publishing imprints. Max and his editorial team had developed an uncanny knack for spotting best-sellers, and the company's turnover had trebled in the last three years. Knowing his target audience as he did, however, Max was not convinced that the details of his brother's planned expedition to a remote island off the coast of Greenland would make a profitable read.

By his side, Max's girlfriend, Anita, toyed with her dessertspoon as Jonathan talked. Max glanced at her, taking in the way the candlelight reflecting from the table softened her profile and cast shadows that emphasised the lush swell of her cleavage. She was a stunningly beautiful woman, with her long, curling fall of Titian hair and her full, sensual mouth, but he had to admit he was becoming somewhat bored with her. She had latched onto him, he suspected, largely for his wealth, and much as he enjoyed showing her off, he was beginning to suspect he wanted more in his life than a pretty hanger-on. God forbid that he was turning into Jonathan, searching for a woman who had ideas of her own and could make a significant contribution to a conversation!

He turned his gaze to the girl sitting opposite him, who had been eagerly making comments on the proposed expedition throughout the meal. Justine McClure was a final-year archaeology student at St Susan's, and Jonathan had declared her to be his brightest pupil. From the fact that they had not asked for separate bedrooms, Max deduced that his brother's interest in her was more than simply academic. For a moment his eyes met Justine's. She looked away, and blushed. Max wondered what Jonathan had told her about his older brother. He suspected it would not have been even remotely flattering.

The two brothers could not, in truth, have been more different. Physically, there was something of a resemblance; both stood six foot in height, and their blue-green eyes and finely-sculpted cheekbones had been inherited from their mother, though where Max was flaxen blond, with a sharp, prominent nose, Jonathan was dark, with more classically-honed features. Temperamentally, Max was fire: impatient, arrogant, driven. Jonathan was more laid-back, unruffled by the little things which would drive Max into a fury. The contrasts in their personalities were highlighted by the way they had chosen to spend the money they had inherited from their grandmother on their respective twenty-first birthdays. Besides setting up his publishing company, Max had invested in art and fine wines, and had built up a business portfolio which would guarantee him a very comfortable middle life and old age. Jonathan, on the other hand, had chosen to use his bequest to fund the archaeological trips which had taken him around the world. He was deep in an explanation of his latest project as Max tuned back into the conversation.

'So they reckon that Odinland is the last undiscovered Viking settlement,' Jonathan was saying, pouring himself another generous glass of Cabernet Sauvignon. 'You see, not everyone who set off for Greenland made it all the way. Some of their ships capsized, others turned back when their supplies began to run out. This island was apparently the last stop-off point en route, and a handful of them decided to stay there, rather than risk the last few hundred miles of the trip. That was back in the tenth century, and the island has been undisturbed ever since.' He paused, and took a sip of wine before continuing.

'Anyway, the settlement began to prosper. The climate was kind to them, and the land was fruitful. But after only a dozen years or so, it was gone; the manuscript I've translated seems to indicate that when a scout party returned to the island from Greenland, they found the village deserted. It's like the Nordic equivalent of the *Marie Celeste* – everything was as though they'd just walked away from it. There were fires burning in the hearths and even a pig in the cooking pot in one of the huts, but there was no sign of a living being anywhere. The scouting party just got back in their boats and fled, claiming the villagers had been taken by the gods for indulging in some unnatural practice, and they never returned. If I'm right, and the island settlement is still intact when we excavate, this could be our best insight ever into how the Vikings used to live.'

'How fascinating,' Anita murmured.

'Well, it just sounds dull to me,' Max replied, trying to keep the boredom out of his voice. 'Rooting round digging up old bones and broken pottery... I've never understood the fascination, Jon.'

'Oh, but this is going to be so much more than just old bones.' Jonathan's eyes glittered with alcohol and excitement. 'This is the whole lot, Max. No one's set foot on that island for a thousand years. We might not have found out about it now, if that team from the Archaeological Trust hadn't dug up that longship on the Yorkshire coast. For some reason that I haven't been able to discover, all the writings on the Odinland settlement had been systematically destroyed; only this one particular manuscript seems to have escaped. It's as though they never wanted anyone to learn what had been happening on the island.'

'You should have seen Jon,' Justine said, suddenly breaking into the conversation. 'He was like a kid with a new toy when they handed him that manuscript to translate. I've never seen him so excited. He was telling me that he always regretted being too young to take part in the dig when they were rescuing the old town of Jorvik from under the streets of York. Well, this is going to be his Jorvik.'

'Not just mine,' Jonathan replied. 'I've been liaising with Dr Adrienne Devaney, over in Boston. The Vikings' attempt to colonise North America is her specialist subject, and she's as excited about this as I am. In fact, I was speaking to her earlier in the week, and I've managed to persuade her to sign up for the expedition.'

Max sighed to himself. His brother's enthusiasm for archaeology seemed infinite, and he could happily ramble on about the subject all night, no matter how much it bored everyone else. The girl, Justine, seemed to share her tutor's passion, and had spoken of him with undisguised admiration throughout the evening. She was a pretty little thing, with her short, straight blonde hair, wide green eyes and elfin features, completely wasted on the academic Jonathan, who could happily go from one year to the next without so much as looking at a woman

9

if there was an obscure parchment to be translated, or a lost tribe to be excavated. Idly, Max wondered whether he might have a chance with Justine himself …

There was a sudden crash, halting Jonathan's speech in mid-flow. Max turned to see Anita gazing at him apologetically. She had risen to her feet and made a tipsy attempt to begin clearing away the dessert dishes, in preparation for the coffee, port and selection of cheeses that was to follow. However, she had only succeeded in dropping one of the delicate crystal bowls that had contained the creamy meringue confection, sending it smashing to the floor in dozens of irreparable shards.

'I – I'm sorry, Max,' Anita began, imploringly, well aware of how her clumsiness would be rewarded.

'You know those bowls belonged to my grandmother,' he retorted. 'I can't just replace them by going down to Habitat, now can I?'

'Yes, I know, but I didn't mean to—'

'Of course you didn't mean to. You never do mean to, do you, you clumsy little slut?' Max realised that both Jonathan and Justine were staring at him in astonishment, and he was aware of how out of proportion his reaction must seem in relation to the trivial incident which had started it. Jonathan, of course, was all too familiar with his brother's quick temper, having been on the receiving end of it many times during childhood, but his girlfriend would never have witnessed it before. And neither of them would know the deeper meaning that lay behind Max's apparently excessive show of anger. Still, his next words would help to make his reasoning clear.

'You know what your clumsiness means, don't you, Anita?' he asked.

'Y-yes,' Anita replied.

'Yes, what?' His voice had lost its sudden edge of anger, which had been replaced with an icy calm and the impression that he was talking to a particularly dim-witted child.

'Yes, Master,' Anita amended.

'And what does it mean?' They had gone through this ritual many times during the course of their relationship, but Max never failed to become excited by the thought of what was to follow. Already he could begin to feel his penis stirring, pressing against the cool dark blue silk of his boxer shorts.

'It means I have to be punished, Master.' Justine was open-mouthed with indignation and seemed ready to speak out; Max could see that Jonathan had placed a restraining hand on her arm, warning her against intervention. Perhaps he's worked out what's happening, Max thought. Perhaps it turns him on as much as it turns me on. We shall see.

'Right then, let's see you strip,' Max ordered. Anita gazed at him mutely, imploring him with her eyes not to force her to do this in front of his invited guests. He merely stared back impassively.

'I shouldn't refuse, if I were you, darling,' he warned her. 'You know the penalties for sluts who refuse to obey an order.'

At this, Anita reached reluctantly behind her, and took hold of the zip on her tight-fitting black cocktail dress. She pulled it down slowly, and let the thin straps of the dress slip from her shoulders. It dropped to the floor in a rustle of heavy taffeta, pooling around her ankles to reveal that, beneath it, Anita was wearing an exquisite scarlet corset, trimmed with black lace. The corset was tightly laced, pulling her waist in to an impossibly tiny size and giving her an idealised hourglass figure. Her large breasts,

11

with their pale apricot nipples, spilled out from above the half-cups of the corset, their alabaster flesh flushing as she failed to hide her humiliation at being asked to undress in front of the guests. This humiliation was compounded by the fact that, this evening, Max had not allowed her to wear any knickers. Both Jonathan and Justine could clearly see her neatly trimmed triangle of flame-red pubic hair, framed and emphasised by the scarlet straps of the suspenders that reached from below the corset to hold up her sheer black stockings.

'Beautiful, isn't she, Jonathan?' Max murmured, coming close to Anita to run a possessive hand down her cheek and on to the bare flesh of her shoulder and breasts. Almost absent-mindedly, he toyed with her nipple, feeling its soft areola begin to stiffen beneath his touch. 'And so very, very obedient.'

Jonathan made no reply, but Max noticed that he was shifting almost imperceptibly in his seat, trying to make himself comfortable. Perhaps his brother was also getting an erection at the thought of Anita receiving her punishment. This would, undoubtedly, be a special moment; though Max had realised within a very short time of getting to know Anita that she had deeply submissive tendencies, and had guided her quickly and skilfully into the role of his obedient slave, he had never been in a position to exhibit her compliance in front of an audience, until now.

'That's good, slut, but not good enough,' he whispered in Anita's ear. 'Next time I give you an order I expect you to obey it instantly, guests or no guests. You know that hesitation will merely earn you a little extra punishment.' He gave her nipple a sudden tweak; not hard, but with just enough force to make her suppress a wince. Turning his back on her, he picked up the chair she had been sitting on, and set it in the middle of the dining-room floor. 'Now, bend over that chair, and display yourself,' he ordered.

This time, there was no hesitation, even though it was all too apparent that Anita did not want to comply with his order. The redhead quickly assumed the desired position, clutching on to the solid wooden chair back with both hands, and spreading her legs about a foot apart. This movement was just enough to expose the hanging pouch of her sex, already beginning to glisten with a little of her intimate moisture. For all that she protested, she was enjoying doing what Max asked of her.

'Wider, slut,' Max said casually. 'Show my brother and his girlfriend that wet little pussy of yours.'

Obediently, Anita widened her stance. The backs of her thighs tautened slightly, as she balanced precariously on the spindle-thin stiletto heels of her shoes. That position would not be comfortable to sustain for a long period of time, Max knew, but he enjoyed seeing the way she would contort her body into whatever pose he desired without demur.

Max reached down between her legs, and ran his index finger the length of her moist slit. When he pulled it away, it was coated with her juices. 'I was right, you are wet,' he observed dispassionately. 'Go on, slut, taste yourself.'

He thrust his finger into her mouth, and she sucked it like a baby might suck a dummy, the wet pressure of her tongue and lips seeming to coax his erection to even greater hardness. Max knew how her feminine essence would taste: tart and salty, spiced with the aroma of her arousal. He wanted to sample it himself, but there would be time enough for that later.

Impatiently, he withdrew his finger from between her lips, glancing at his guests to gauge their reaction. His brother was rapt with attention, chin cupped in his palms and the little finger of his right hand in his mouth. Beside him, Justine's cheeks were flushing red, but she did not look away from the spectacle. Perhaps she could not believe what she was seeing.

'So how many strokes did we agree?' Max asked Anita.

'I don't think we did, Master,' she replied timidly.

'How many should we make it?' He savoured for a moment the power of knowing that, whatever he decided, she would not argue. Arguing would only earn her a couple more slaps across that taut, peachy arse, already quivering as she anticipated the punishment to come. 'Jon, what do you think?'

Jonathan looked at him, startled. 'I – er – six?' he suggested hopefully. No doubt he was remembering the headmistress at their prep school, Miss Montague. Punishment, when she had dispensed it, had consisted of six sharp strokes on a boy's outstretched palm with an old wooden ruler, which she had referred to as 'the chastiser'. Max had succumbed to its fiery sting on two occasions, his brother only once, but neither of them had forgotten its pain. More frightening, in Max's memory, had been the long minutes when she had searched for the much-used implement, and tapped it smartly against her own palm, prolonging the moment when it would be employed. It had left in Max the curious urge to discover how it would feel if the positions were reversed: if he was the one who dispensed pain, rather than received it. In his adult life he had known that feeling many times, and it had never failed to leave him less than gratified.

'Six? For a bowl of that value and those cheeky, insolent

remarks?' Max replied, more for Anita's benefit than Jonathan's.

Jonathan glanced at his brother, and then at Justine. 'Okay, make it a dozen, then.'

'Very well, a dozen it is,' Max said. He ran a caressing hand over Anita's corset-clad back and down to the twin taut globes beneath. 'Six with the hand, and six with the belt.'

Anita made as if to rise from her bent-over position, but the look Max gave her stilled her protest.

'Now, count and thank me after each one, slut,' he ordered. 'If you forget, I shall have to start again. Is that understood?'

'Yes, Master.'

Max raised his hand. In that moment, there was silence in the room, broken only by the distant ticking of the grandfather clock in the hall outside. He brought his palm sharply down, connecting with Anita's right cheek.

'One, thank you, Master,' Anita muttered.

The first smack was followed swiftly by a second, this time on her left cheek. Again, the submissive Anita thanked her Master, though there was more of a pause before she spoke. This procedure was repeated four more times in quick succession, Max's blows falling hard enough to leave clear red imprints of his palm on her pale skin. Anita was biting her lip at every slap, her hair had fallen over her face in disarray, one of her breasts had come completely free from her corset and her eyes were glistening with tears of humiliation.

Unhurriedly, Max stepped away from her, unbuckled his belt and drew it out of the loops in his dark trousers. He hefted it lovingly in his hand for a second. It was made of finest Spanish leather, an inch wide and beautifully supple. Max doubled the belt on itself and wound it around his palm, making sure he clutched the buckle so it could do no damage to Anita's delicate flesh.

Again he inspected Anita's sex with probing fingers. There was a noticeable increase in her juices, and her outer labia were puffy and swollen with need.

He caught hold of her tumbled curls, and brought her face up to meet his gaze. The shame and excitement she was experiencing was evident in her expression. 'That was just the appetiser, slut,' he informed her. 'Are you ready for the main course?'

'Yes, Master,' she replied obediently.

'So we begin again at seven,' he said. The belt hovered in the air for a moment, then descended on Anita's backside. Her fingers gripped convulsively at the chair back, her knuckles whitening, but she did not cry out.

'Seven, thank you, Master,' she said in a small, strangled voice, even as a wide red welt began to appear across both buttocks. Max placed the next one a little higher, careful not to pile pain upon pain; after all, there were still another four strokes to be endured.

'Eight, thank you, Master.'

He ran an experimental finger over the raised marks the belt had caused, then dipped his finger down between the cheeks of Anita's arse and on into her moist furrow. He lingered on her clit until she began to relax into the rhythm of his rubbing, at which point he immediately withdrew.

The belt came down again, this time on the fleshy underhang of her cheeks. She yelped, then recovered sufficiently to thank him. Again he stroked her clit and she shuddered at his touch. He knew from experience that it did not take much to bring her to orgasm once the pain in her punished buttocks had begun to transmute itself to pleasure, but he delighted in frustrating her for as long as he could.

The tenth stroke was aimed at the tops of her thighs. There had been no hand spanking there to warm the flesh, and Anita shot upright, rubbing furiously at the sore place. 'Ten, thank you, Master,' she sobbed, having retained enough presence of mind to prevent him beginning her punishment afresh.

He gave her the last two strokes on top of the ones he had already administered, knowing that the mounting pain would serve only to heighten her arousal. This time, when his finger skimmed her clit, she thrust her backside out lewdly, eagerly, reminding him of a bitch on heat. It took only seconds for him to coax a climax from her, and he pushed his thumb inside, feeling her inner muscles pulsate around it as she orgasmed. Max's imagination raced, and for a moment it was Justine who stood before him, naked from the waist down, her arse viciously striped and her quim open and saturated, ready for him to slide his cock inside.

It was Justine's voice that broke his reverie. 'I really think I should be going to bed,' she said.

Yes, you should be going to my bed, Max wanted to tell her, picturing her tied, spread-eagled and face down, to its four posts, with no idea which of her orifices he would penetrate first. The thought was causing his cock to pulse almost painfully, aching for relief, and he muttered absently, 'Aren't you going to stay for coffee?'

'No. Thank you, but no.' She turned and prepared to flee from the room. He caught her arm as she tried to pass him.

'Just stay long enough to hear me out,' he urged. 'You want me to endorse my brother's expedition, well, I shall.

On one condition.'

'And what's that?' Justine asked, pulling free of his grasp.

'That I'm part of the team he takes with him. What do you say, Jon?' he asked, watching his brother rise to his feet. 'You'll take me to Odinland, won't you?'

'I can have my book contract?' Jonathan replied.

'Of course.'

'That's brilliant.' Jonathan embraced Max, a grin of delight splitting his face. He hugged Justine too, and then took her hand and headed for the door. He turned and looked back at his brother. 'Thanks, Max. I'll never be able to repay you.'

Max watched them disappear up to bed. Oh, but you will, he thought, turning his attention back to Anita, who still clutched the chair back limply, not having been given permission to rise. Or, rather, your lovely little girlfriend will. As he freed his cock from his trousers, stroking his straining length, his thoughts were only of Justine. He plunged his full length fiercely into Anita's gaping pussy, causing her to cry out. He was glad she could not see his face, or realise that, although he was thrusting into a beautiful, voluptuous redhead, his thoughts were only for the girlish blonde he intended to steal from his brother. Sensing his imminent climax, he pulled out of Anita's clinging channel to allow his seed to splash over her ravaged buttocks. Don't thank me, Jonathan, he gasped inwardly as he came; by the time this expedition is over, you may regret ever allowing me to tag along.

Chapter Two

Justine rose early the following morning, unable to sleep. Beside her, Jonathan was snoring gently, his face turned towards her and his soft, dark hair falling appealingly on to his forehead. She smiled to herself. She could lie happily for hours, watching him sleep, still unable to believe that this kind, intelligent, stunningly attractive man was hers. Idly, she thought back to the first year of her university course, when she had spent most of Jonathan's lectures gazing rapt at the handsome archaeologist, and fantasising about what it would be like to make love with him, his body covering hers and his cock deep inside her. She had paid so little attention to what he had actually been saying that when she had gained the second highest marks in the end-of-year exams, no one had been more surprised than herself. That surprise had only been topped by the one she had received when he had invited her to dinner in his flat following that exam success. After that night she had only returned to her own lodgings to pick up her clothes and books, and Jonathan had become her first – and only – serious lover.

For a moment she thought about squirming down under the covers and taking his penis in her mouth, licking it till it hardened and he woke with an eagerness to fuck her. It was a nice idea, and one she would have pursued if she had not been quite so hungry. No one who saw her slender figure believed that Justine could eat quite as much as she did. She blessed her luck and put it down to a fast metabolism, aware of the envious glances of friends who had to eat carefully and exercise on a regular basis if they wanted to keep their weight down.

Quietly, she slipped out of bed without waking Jonathan and dressed in a soft blue chambray shirt worn loose over black jeans. This was an outfit she felt comfortable in; last night she had dressed for dinner in a short, bottle-green crushed velvet dress that showed off her long, slim legs, but she much preferred to roam around in old, casual clothes which were practical for her studies and field trips. She could never have been happy in anything as elaborate and constricting as the corset Anita had worn the night before.

Thinking of Anita, and the punishment Max had inflicted on her, was unsettling. Justine could not believe how the woman had submitted so willingly to being thrashed and fingered in that manner. She tried not to acknowledge the part of her which was wondering how it would feel if she had been the one who had been made to strip and display herself, before Max had drawn a climax from her body with his mixture of slaps and caresses. But why was she even thinking of that man touching her, let alone stimulating her so intimately?

Jonathan had been right: he and his brother were nothing alike. Max might have been as attractive as Jonathan on the surface, but he was cold-hearted, and only interested in his own selfish pleasure. Though she could not deny that Anita had enjoyed everything which had been done to her. Justine shook her head, trying to clear it of conflicting thoughts, and crept out of the bedroom. Once outside on the landing she pulled on her favourite pair of battered leather boots, and went in search of the kitchen.

She still found it hard to believe that Max Cavendish had agreed to join Jonathan's expedition and commission the resulting story. All the way over in the car from Oxford, Jonathan had told her how Max would listen with polite interest and then turn him down flat. And that had certainly seemed to be the case, at least for the first part of last evening. What had happened to make him change his mind?

Justine managed to remember her way through the maze of rooms in the house. Max had told them that breakfast would be an informal meal, and that as he would more than likely be having a lie-in, she and Jonathan were to make themselves at home. Though this house was as unlike home as Justine, who had been brought up in a small two-up, two-down house in a Midlands mining village, could imagine. It was obvious from the work Max had done on the farmhouse that he was wealthy, but there were no signs of ostentation in the decor. Everything that had been done to the house was completely in keeping with its original design and structure. Whatever else she thought about Max Cavendish, she could not deny that the man had good taste.

Someone – Anita, Justine presumed – had set four places at the pine kitchen table, the bowls, plates and mugs all in the familiar blue-and-white willow pattern. A cafetiere stood on one of the work surfaces, close to the kettle, and Justine busied herself grinding beans in the wooden coffee mill, before setting water to boil. She was hunting through cupboards, looking more in hope than in expectation far a packet of cornflakes, when she heard someone cough behind her. She turned, to see Max standing in the kitchen doorway, dressed in an Aran sweater and a pair of faded jeans, his blond hair damp from the shower.

He smiled and walked towards her. 'Good morning, Justine. I trust you slept well.'

Something in his tone compelled Justine to honesty. 'No, not really. If you must know, I was rather upset by what happened last night.'

'Really?' He raised an eyebrow, quizzically, and she was struck by how much his long-lashed, blue-green eyes were like his brother's. His gaze was almost hypnotic; she found it hard to tear her eyes away. 'The kettle's boiling,' he said, quietly. 'Why don't you make the coffee, and then we can talk about why you were upset.'

You know damn well why, Justine wanted to reply, but she was wary of annoying the quick-tempered Max. Instead, she poured water into the cafetiere, and waited for the coffee to brew.

'What do you fancy for breakfast?' Max asked conversationally. 'Bacon? Eggs? Toast?'

'Please,' Justine replied, her anger at Max briefly forgotten. She sat at the table, sipping her coffee and watching as he went through the motions of preparing breakfast for the two of them. Soon the delicious smell of frying bacon filled the sunny kitchen.

'Jonathan's pretty handy when it comes to cooking,' she muttered, as Max cracked golden-yoked eggs and added them to the pan. 'That's part of his appeal. I got bored with going out with lads who just about know how to heat up a tin of soup.'

Max placed a plate of bacon and eggs before Justine. 'So did you have many boyfriends before Jonathan?' he asked, trying to sound as though he was not prying.

'One or two,' she replied, attacking her breakfast with gusto. 'They were nothing in comparison to Jon, though.'

She ate with relish, wiping her plate clean with one half

of the round of toast Max had given her, then smearing the other half with home-made damson jam. She was aware of Max watching her as she licked her fingers clean of butter and toast crumbs.

'Is something wrong?' she asked.

He smiled. 'I just like to see a woman with a healthy appetite.' He poured more coffee into Justine's mug. 'Now, why don't you tell me what it was that upset you so much last night?'

Justine sighed, wondering where to begin. Finally she said, 'I can't believe what a bastard you were to Anita. Okay, so she smashed your precious bowl, but it was an accident. She certainly didn't deserve to have all those things done to her. Especially not in front of Jon and me.'

'Oh, Justine, you really don't understand, do you?' Max replied, refilling his own mug. 'That's the sort of relationship Anita and I have. She submits to my desires, and she does so willingly. It's an agreement: there are certain rules, therefore she does deserve what she gets if she transgresses them.'

'But how can she bear to have you make her do such degrading things? If it was me, I wouldn't undress in front of other people, or let you spank me, or touch me like that.'

'That's where you're wrong.' Max fixed her with an enigmatic gaze. 'I've known girls like you before Justine. Bright, sparky girls with a good brain, a pretty face and an independent streak. They sit there, just like you, and they tell me how they wouldn't let a man treat them like this, that, or the other. And yet I know damn well that deep down, that's exactly how they want to be treated.'

'That's crap, and you know it.' Justine was indignant. How could this arrogant, overbearing man even presume to tell her how she felt?

'I don't think so.' He pulled his chair close to hers, so that their knees were almost touching, and stared at her intently. She was aware of the scent of his freshly-washed hair and the healthy, male smell of his skin. 'For all your protestations, there's part of you that would love to have me telling you what to do. Think about it, Justine. Imagine I ordered you to walk down a busy street near your college, wearing no knickers and a skirt that would fly up at the merest breeze. Or I made you spread your legs wide and play with yourself like a slut. Or I tied you to the bed and pushed a big, fat candle into your tight little quim. Tell me the thought of that doesn't turn you on.'

'I—' Justine began, aware that something in Max's tone – for it surely could not have been the images he described – was making her skin flush and her sex pulsate. She could not raise her eyes to meet his gaze, afraid of what she might see reflected there.

'Does Jonathan ever suggest anything like that to you?' Max enquired.

'Of course not. He wouldn't treat me like that.'

'Why don't you come with me, and I'll show you something?' Max rose to his feet and gestured to Justine to follow him. 'There's part of the house I didn't take you to last night. I thought at the time you might not appreciate it, but I've changed my mind since then.'

Against her better judgement, Justine let Max lead her up the stairs and along the corridor, past the bedrooms where Jonathan and, presumably, Anita still lay sleeping. At the end of the pile-carpeted passageway was a small, white-painted door. Justine had noticed it the previous night, and merely assumed it to be a cupboard of some kind. Now she wondered what kind of secret it would

24

reveal.

Max pulled a keychain from his pocket and sought through the selection of keys on it. Having found the one he was looking for he slotted it into the keyhole and turned it. The door swung open, soundlessly.

'Come in, then,' Max said, adding as Justine hesitated, 'there's nothing to be afraid of. I'm not Bluebeard; I haven't got all my old girlfriends hanging up in here.'

Cautiously, Justine went inside, and found herself in a low-ceilinged, black-painted room. There were no carpets and the room was bare of furniture, apart from a high stool with a padded top, and what, curiously, appeared to be a pillory. Lengths of chain hung from hooks in one wall, and there was a rack on another bearing a collection of implements; Justine recognised among them a couple of canes of the type that old-fashioned schoolteachers had used, and a dimpled table-tennis bat. She did not dare to speculate on what some of the others might be.

'So do you like my playroom?' Max asked.

'I'm not even going to begin to ask what sort of games you play in here,' Justine replied. She expected Max to turn and lead her out of the room, but instead he pushed the door firmly shut behind him.

'This is your chance to find out, little Justine,' he said, walking over to her. 'Why don't you investigate some of the things in here a little more closely?'

'What, stick my head in the pillory and let you use some of those things on me?' She retorted, gesturing to Max's collection of punishment implements. 'Not likely.'

'Don't worry, I wouldn't use half of those on a beginner like you.' Max reached out and stroked her cheek gently. 'I know you think I'm some kind of vicious bully, but you'll change your mind once you get to know me.'

'I've got no intention of getting to know you,' Justine told him firmly.

'Well, that's going to be a little bit difficult if we're going to be stuck on Fantasy Island with my brother this summer. Come on, little Justine…' his voice was soft, like a caress, '…aren't you at all interested in finding out why Anita submits to me the way she does?'

'Well…'

'Let me show you the cuffs. They'll prove that I don't hurt Anita.' He led Justine over to the wall from which the chains hung. On the end of one section of chain was a pair of leather wrist cuffs, padded with sheepskin. 'Most people use metal cuffs, but they can chafe. Just feel the softness of these.' Lured on by his sensual voice, Justine did as she was commanded. She had to admit that the thick fleece did feel soft to the touch. 'Try them on,' Max wheedled. 'Just as an experiment.'

Obediently, Justine held out her wrists and let Max shackle them with the cuffs. It was only as he snapped them shut and fastened the small lock on each one that her mind flicked back to full awareness, and she realised that she was now effectively his prisoner.

'Okay, Max, that's enough.' Her voice was edgy, though she reassured herself with the knowledge that both Anita and Jonathan were within hailing distance. Though God knew what Jonathan would say when she told him she had been stupid enough to let Max cuff her wrists.

'Oh, Justine, you disappoint me. I thought you were more adventurous than this. I mean, don't you want to find out what happens when I do this…?' He began to turn a winch on the wall, and Justine found her wrists being jerked upwards until her hands were above her head. Max kept turning until the chain clicked into place and

Justine found herself on tiptoe, her back pressed flat against the wall of his mock dungeon.

'Max, please,' Justine begged. A joke was a joke, but this was going too far. Perhaps this was his way of getting back at her for her comments in the kitchen, but if he wanted to teach her the lesson that she was not to cross him, she was already satisfied that she had learned it well enough.

'Please what?' Max asked. 'Please let me go, or please carry on?' As he spoke he reached out and undid the top button of her chambray shirt. Justine shivered, trying to fight the effect that Max's words and his slow, deliberate actions were having on her. She tried to convince herself that if she had woken Jonathan and cajoled him into having sex with her, she would not now be feeling the ache of desire gnawing at her womb.

'I must say, you've gone very quiet,' Max commented, unfastening the next button. The shirt now gaped sufficiently that the tops of her small breasts must be apparent to him. Justine tried not to imagine what he would see if he opened the next one, all the while wondering why she was eager for him to do so. 'What happened to the girl in the kitchen who had an answer for everything and told me that what I was doing was wrong?' He pressed his mouth to her ear and whispered, 'Could it be that she's realised I was actually right?'

'No,' Justine muttered, as he opened two more buttons in quick succession.

'I didn't think you wore a bra,' Max said, 'although I have to say that was fairly obvious last night, when I was punishing Anita. Did you know quite how prominent your nipples become when you're excited, Justine? Just like they are now…' He dispensed quickly with the last few buttons, and reached into her open shirt to stroke her breasts.

'You've got lovely little tits, Justine, although I expect my brother's told you that often enough.' His hands moulded and caressed the firm mounds, eliciting a moan from Justine. 'You know I could do absolutely anything I wanted to you now, and you have no way of stopping me.'

'I could kick you,' Justine replied, trying to fight the sensations of pleasure Max's hands were creating in her sensitive nipples.

'Not if I cuffed your ankles as well,' he said, matter-of-factly. 'I might do that. Spread your legs so wide I can touch you everywhere. How would you like that?'

'Oh, Max.' Justine sighed, unbearably aroused despite his threats, and ashamed of herself for becoming so turned on. This man had tricked her into bondage and was flagrantly abusing not only her body, but his relationship with his own brother. How could she feel the least desire for him, or extract any enjoyment from what he was doing? And yet she knew that if only his hands would keep playing those wicked games with her nipples, she would let him do anything.

Abruptly, he turned his attention to the belt that cinched her jeans. 'How about if I spread your legs, and then let Jon and Anita watch while I frigged you?'

'No!' she gasped, desire fading at the suggestion. 'Please, Max, I don't want them to see you doing this to me.'

'You're still assuming that you have a choice, aren't you?' Her belt was undone, and now he was working on the zip of her jeans. 'If I decide that Jon's going to see you hanging here while I finger-fuck you, then that's exactly what's going to happen.'

Justine closed her eyes. The thought of her boyfriend watching while his brother masturbated her to a climax was too humiliating to contemplate, but she could not deny that if he appeared in the doorway at this moment, she would be unable to ask Max to stop.

Max pushed her jeans down off her narrow hips. Now all that shielded her modesty from him was a pair of white lacy knickers. He could not fail to notice that they were already damp with her excitement.

'I know you love my brother,' Max said, almost absent-mindedly, 'but I doubt that he's ever going to be able to satisfy you properly. Not now you're beginning to realise how submissive you really are. He's a sweet boy, but Jon just isn't the dominant type, believe me.'

'And how submissive am I?' Justine asked, still driven by the urge to fight against him.

'Oh, you're as submissive as they come, Justine, if only you'd acknowledge the fact. Wait till we're alone on Odinland together. By the time I've finished with you, if I tell you to crawl on the floor, you'll be crawling on the floor. I'm going to have you begging me to fuck you in every orifice.'

As he spoke he rested his hand on the gentle curve of her stomach. Justine whimpered as his hands began to slide down under the waistband of her knickers.

'You could tell me to stop,' Max observed. 'I mean, I may like to dominate women, but I don't get a kick out of forcing them to do anything they don't want to. But you want this, don't you?'

His fingers moved lower, stroking her soft pubic hair and parting the swollen lips beneath. He was watching her intently, she knew that, but Justine could not meet his penetrating blue-green gaze. She was torn between the shame of being fondled by him in this way, and the shame of knowing that she was enjoying it. In unspoken answer to his question, she eased her legs apart slightly, allowing him easier access to the folds and crevices of her sex.

Her nipples were twin hard points, craving the feel of his mouth. Almost as if he had read her thoughts, Max bent his head and took one rosy peak between his teeth, nipping it with a strength that bordered on pain. His fingers dabbled in the juice that flowed freely between her legs, and then his thumb began to rub at her clitoris with a light, insistent pressure.

'You can't do this to me, Max,' she whispered.

'Why not, little Justine?' he replied. 'You can't pretend you don't like it.' As he spoke he slipped first one finger, then a second, into her gaping channel. 'Doesn't this prove it?'

'Yes.' The word was almost wrung from her lips. 'But Jonathan...'

'If Jonathan had any sense he'd be doing this to you himself. He never learns.'

Justine gasped, partly in reaction to the way Max's fingers were stretching her inner muscles, and partly with the sudden realisation that she was not the first of Jonathan's girlfriends who had succumbed to his brother's seductive, decadent charm.

Max paused in his exploration of her body. 'Did you hear something?' he asked.

Justine, dazed with arousal, shook her head. Max's thumb was no longer stroking her clit, and she found herself moving against his stationary hand, propelling herself towards her imminent climax. She glanced up briefly to see a wolfish smile on his face, and she knew he had triumphed in this battle of wills. Half an hour ago, she had told him she would never let him touch her and now here she was, masturbating herself on his hand.

He spread his fingers a little wider as her sex began to pulse with orgasmic spasms, mimicking the swelling of a cock that was close to orgasm, and she gyrated even more frantically, surrendering to the pleasure that coursed through her body.

What Max might have done to her next, she never knew, for at that moment there was a scream from behind him. He turned his head, and Justine opened her pleasure-glazed eyes to see Anita standing in the doorway.

'Max. You bastard!' Anita screeched.

'Shut the door, you stupid slut,' he hissed back. 'I don't want Jonathan to see this.'

'No, I can imagine why. How could you do this to me? With *her*…' She flung an accusing glare at Justine's suspended, almost naked body, but did as she was ordered, slamming the door. Even fuelled by righteous fury, Anita could not break the habit of obeying Max.

Anita rushed at Max, fingers drawn into claws that would scratch at his cheeks and eyes. He caught hold of her wrists with imperious ease, holding her as she struggled against him. She was attempting to rake her feet down his shins, but in the flat-soled slippers she wore she could do him little damage.

Max hauled her over to the pillory as she attempted to escape his grasp. She was not a small woman, but she did not have the strength to wriggle free. First her left wrist, then her right, was placed in the hand holds, Max holding her securely around the waist with one arm, and then her head was pushed down so that her neck rested in the central groove. Justine suspected that, if Anita really

31

wished to, she could resist and break free, but she realised that the high colour in the redhead's cheeks and the glitter in her eyes was not entirely due to anger. Being manhandled so roughly by Max was turning Anita on.

He slammed the wooden bar of the pillory down, pinioning his girlfriend tightly but not uncomfortably, and snapping shut the heavy steel padlock that kept it in place. Justine wondered whether the piece of equipment had been made to measure, and found herself speculating on how it would accommodate her more slender wrists and neck. She was aware that Max had positioned Anita so that her back was to Justine; he obviously intended her to watch closely as the impending punishment was administered.

For a moment Max pondered the array of implements which hung on the wall, no doubt deciding which to use, and then a better idea came to him. He grabbed one of Anita's ankles and lifted her foot off the floor.

'What are you doing?' she spluttered, as he pulled off her slipper before releasing his hold on her foot.

He flexed the slipper, contemplating its thick rubber sole, a smile of pure malice on his face. 'Perfect,' he breathed. Justine had no idea how much it would hurt to be spanked with a slipper, but from the way Anita was shifting from foot to foot, she sensed that it would not be a pleasant experience.

'You can't do this to me, you bastard,' Anita was repeating.

'You know I can do anything I want,' Max replied coolly.

Justine remembered Max's words: 'I don't force women to do anything they don't want to do'. Did Anita really want this punishment? If she didn't, would Max stop?

'One last thing before we begin,' Max said, and picked

up the hem of Anita's short slip of a nightdress. He pulled it up so it was bunched around her neck, leaving her body completely exposed to his own and Justine's gaze. He fondled her body almost casually, twisting her pale nipples and tugging on her heavy, hanging breasts. She squealed at the rough treatment, but her posture seemed to be encouraging him.

At last Max tired of this and moved to stand behind her. Unlike the ritualised punishment of the night before, he did not inform her of the number of strokes, or request her to count them. He simply began to pepper her backside with a volley of rapid slaps from the slipper. He worked steadily and methodically, making sure that no inch of her ample arse cheeks remained untouched, and as his hand came down repeatedly, so her flesh began to change colour from an unblemished porcelain white to a mottled, angry-looking red.

Anita was soon sobbing, begging Max to go easy on her, but he seemed deaf to her pleas. He turned his attention lower, spanking the tops of her thighs with the same even thoroughness. When she tried to pull away from the slipper's next descent, he simply caught her by the waist and held her steady.

Justine could see the outline of Max's cock, curving along his thigh where the thick denim prevented it from rising to erection, and she smelt a spicy female excitement in the air which was not her own. She was disturbed to find that her feelings towards the spanking she was witnessing had changed: she was no longer indignant on Anita's behalf at the length and severity of the punishment she was receiving. Instead, she wanted to be held by the combination of the wooden pillory and Max's strong left arm while her own backside was pelted with the slipper's tough rubber sole. She twisted frustratedly in her bondage, rubbing her thighs together in an attempt to give her clit the stimulation it demanded.

At last, the fusillade of slaps on Anita's rump was reaching its climax. She was still squirming and moaning, but now these were gasps of throaty excitement, rather than pain. Justine could not quite see what Max's left hand was doing, but she suspected it had wormed its way into the depths of Anita's pussy, and he was frigging his girlfriend as he had frigged her just a little earlier.

Anita gave one last cry and convulsed against Max's hand, then hung limply, her body shuddering as she fought to regain control of her breathing. Max released his grip on her almost contemptuously, and threw the slipper to the floor. He unlocked the pillory and watched dispassionately as she rearranged the nightdress to cover herself.

'You're too easy, slut,' he remarked. 'You're just not enough of a challenge any more.'

'Yes, I know, you've told me that often enough,' Anita responded, 'and do you know what? You're right. I'm easy because you've made me easy, Max. All you have to do is threaten to spank me and I get wet. You don't know how I really feel, what I really think: I'm just another expensive plaything of yours, like everything else in this house. Well, it doesn't matter any more. I've had enough. I'm not going to stay here and let you humiliate me any further. You can go play Indiana Jones with your brother for all I care. I'm leaving you, Max, and I'm going to find a Master who'll care about me more than he cares about himself.' She shot one last furious look at Justine as she stalked out of the playroom. 'He'll do just the same to you if you're stupid enough to let him, you know,' she muttered, running a hand down Justine's cheek. 'Break your will, get you hooked on him, and then dump you for a fresh victim. I pity you, I really do.'

The door slammed behind the departing Anita with a hollow sound, leaving Justine alone with Max. As he came towards her, Justine hoped that he would continue with her body where he had left off, but he simply lowered the hanging chain until her feet were on solid ground once more, and unfastened the handcuffs.

'Are you going to talk her out of it?' Justine asked, buttoning her shirt.

Max simply fixed her with an unreadable look, turned on his heel and left. Justine stared after him. His girlfriend had just walked out on him after shooting his reputation down in flames; surely he should be showing some kind of emotion. She could not understand why he simply did not seem to care. She struggled into the rest of her clothes, Anita's warning ringing in her ears. Well, Max Cavendish would never break her will. She could never get hooked on such a man, she told herself sternly, not while Jonathan was around. She almost succeeded in ignoring the little inner voice that whispered, 'That's what you think.'

Chapter Three

The afternoon sun slanted in through the window of her study as Dr Adrienne Devaney completed the last of her paperwork for the academic year. In another half an hour or so she would be able to power down her word processor, lock the door behind her, and turn her back on Harvard and the university town of Cambridge, Massachusetts, for the rest of the summer.

This was always the most boring part of teaching, as far as she was concerned: marking and grading papers was a necessary evil that kept her away from her twin loves of lecturing and researching, but having to keep files on all her students that detailed their social and psychological well-being as well as their academic process seemed nothing more than a waste of time.

Adrienne had been finding it particularly difficult to concentrate on this afternoon's work. This was partly due to the fact that her mind was racing ahead to the forthcoming archaeological dig in Odinland. Ever since Jon Cavendish had contacted her and made a tentative approach towards her becoming part of his expedition, she had been able to think of little else. Like him, she was fascinated with the mystique of the abandoned island, and wanted nothing more than to step on to its soil and discover the truth for herself. It would be the culmination of years of hard work, and if any significant findings were unearthed, they could only strengthen her standing in what was still a largely male-dominated area of study, where the theses and ideas of women were routinely considered to be of less academic value than those of men.

Not that she was any stranger to prejudice, she thought ruefully, catching a glimpse of her reflection in the screen of her monitor. As a woman of mixed race, she knew she would have gained more respect among black academics by studying Afro-American traditions, rather than becoming a lecturer in Norse mythology and culture. The truth was that her university career and field of study had been chosen in memory of her Norwegian father, Per. He had defied his family by marrying her mother, Marla, a young black girl from Harlem who he had met while working in New York City, and had lavished love and attention on his wife and their daughter for seven years, before he had been killed in a traffic accident. Marla had remarried, and Adrienne had been made to take the surname of her stepfather. By studying Scandinavian folklore, she had kept alive in her heart her real father and the bedtime stories he had told her: tales of supernaturally brave warriors, mischievous gods and blood-curdling monsters.

When Adrienne had been offered the post of senior lecturer in Scandinavian Studies at Harvard, she had snatched at the chance. It enabled her to live in the refined, slightly old-fashioned city of Boston, where she had an apartment in a redbrick mansion in the wealthy Back Bay district. She loved the strangely English ambience of the town, and the bars and cafes in the theatre district where she often went to relax after a hard day's teaching. With so many colleges in the area, the city was always thronged with students, many of them doing bartering work to help pay for their tuition, and it was not uncommon for her to find herself being served by one of her own pupils.

It had often been remarked that Dr Devaney enjoyed a more intimate relationship with her tutees than most of the other members of staff, and this did not stop at socialising with them. The odd female student would find herself indulging in extra tuition of a more carnal kind, though this was a closely kept secret between Adrienne and the chosen few; if it became generally known that this particular corner of such a highbrow Ivy League establishment was home to sexual deviations the average straight A scholar could never have dreamed of, she was certain to be dismissed instantly.

There was one such scholar in the room even now, and that was the second reason why Adrienne was finding it difficult to concentrate on her work. For the last thirty minutes or so, Casey McGill, who had finished with the third highest grade average in this year's class, had been crouching unseen beneath her tutor's desk, applying the point of her little pink tongue to the soles and heels of Dr Devaney's patent stilettos.

Adrienne pressed the 'save' command on her keyboard and relaxed back in her chair. 'I think you can stop, now, Casey,' she muttered.

'Thank you, Mistress,' the girl replied, with lips that were dry from having lavished so much spittle on her tutor's shoes. She made to crawl out from beneath the desk, but Adrienne nudged her gently with one spiked heel, motioning her back into place.

'Did I say you could get up?' Adrienne asked.

'No, Mistress,' Casey admitted.

'It's very presumptuous of you, isn't it, Casey?' The question was a rhetorical one, and both of them knew it.

'Perhaps I should punish you for that presumption.'

Adrienne's gaze flickered across the room, landing on the wooden-backed chair her pupils usually occupied during one-to-one tutorial sessions. Currently, the only things on that chair were Casey's short tartan skirt, white sweatshirt, cream cotton bra and matching knickers. The girl had stripped seconds after walking into the room, as her Mistress always demanded. All she was permitted to wear were her sneakers and white ankle socks, and a black leather collar that Adrienne had snapped around her neck and buckled securely at the beginning of their session together.

'Yes, I shall punish you,' she decided finally, 'but not just yet. The anticipation will make it all the sweeter for you, won't it? And anyway, I haven't finished with your services yet. I need that busy little tongue of yours somewhere else.'

As she spoke, she let her thighs loll open slightly. The skirt she was wearing was short and flared, and if Casey had cared to glance up, she would have seen that her mistress wore no underwear beneath it, and that the tight, dark petals of her sex were already beginning to unfurl with excitement. 'You know what to do. Get busy.'

Casey's curly brown head disappeared up Adrienne's skirt with satisfying rapidity. The professor parted her thighs wider as she felt the girl's tongue begin to lap at her moist, secret places. Casey, who had had no experience of lesbian lovemaking when she had first started attending Scandinavian Studies classes, was now as knowledgeable about how to make another woman come as she was about tenth-century Viking sagas. Adrienne sighed with pleasure, feeling Casey's lips close around her swollen clitoris and begin to suck eagerly. Low orgasmic pulses rocked her lower body, building a hunger for more. If she so ordered, Casey would lick her to climax three or four times, never expecting to receive any pleasure in return.

Adrienne closed her eyes and threw her head back, twisting and pinching her own nipples through the layers of clothing she wore. She could feel the hard teats of her full, heavy breasts standing proud beneath her silky top and lace bra, and longed to raise them to her own mouth and suckle on them.

A second orgasm shot through her, more powerful than the first, and she thrust Casey's head away abruptly. It was pleasant enough to have one of her little slaves bring her off, but it was equally pleasant to watch them abase and humiliate themselves, submitting to whatever punishment she chose to inflict on them.

'Get up, now, Casey,' she ordered, watching as the girl emerged from beneath the desk, love juices glistening wetly around her mouth and on her chin, 'and go and stand in the window.'

'But – but Mistress, someone might see me,' Casey exclaimed in alarm, glancing down at her own naked body. The study room was on the second floor of the low building, and it was indeed quite possible that someone might gaze out from across the quadrangle, or look up to catch a glimpse of Casey standing nude in the casement.

'You should have thought of that before you presumed to act without being given your orders,' Adrienne said, feigning disinterest.

She watched as the girl slowly made her way across the room, using one hand to shield her pert, rose-tipped breasts and the other to hide her light brown bush.

'Clasp your hands together behind your back,' Adrienne

said. 'If anyone is looking, I want them to get a good view of your tits and pussy.'

Casey did as she was told, her face flushing as she gazed out of the window, looking for passers-by. She made a pretty picture, with her long, slender legs and firm, round buttocks which bore the delightful contrast of pale bikini marks against lightly-tanned flesh, and Adrienne was driven by a sudden desire to bring the girl further discomfort.

'Play with yourself,' she ordered.

Casey shot round and gave her a mortified look. 'Oh please, Mistress, you surely can't mean it. I couldn't possibly…'

'Oh yes, you could,' Adrienne replied. 'And you will, if you don't want an even worse punishment. Do it, Casey; let those passers-by see you fingering your snatch.'

Adrienne smiled with satisfaction as the naked brunette unclasped her hands and moved one slowly round to the front of her body. Casey was tall, and the window sill was just low enough that her crotch would be visible to those outside. Adrienne herself could not quite see what Casey was doing, but she could picture the girl's fingers busily at work between the fleecy curls that covered her pubic mound, and she could hear the low, rhythmic panting that betrayed Casey's arousal. Adrienne knew that despite her student's obvious shame at what she was being made to do, she was excited, too; the submissive streak which surfaced in Casey during these sessions fed on being pressed into ever more humiliating situations.

Casey's legs had parted slightly, and her head was tipped back as she continued to play with herself; she no longer seemed to care whether or not she could be seen from outside. Adrienne could feel her own sex pulsing as she watched the girl bring her other hand up to squeeze her nipples.

'Casey, stop that at once!' she commanded abruptly.

As if she had been shot, Casey dropped both hands and spun round to look at her mistress. Her face was flushed and her nipples were swollen, standing away from their pinkish-brown areolae. A slow trail of arousal trickled stickily down her thighs, and Adrienne realised how close the girl had been to orgasm.

'Come here.' Adrienne patted her lap, and Casey trotted over meekly. 'You know what to do, don't you?'

It was a rhetorical question; Casey was already positioning herself over her mistress' lap. She bent over, so that the flats of her palms were touching the floor; she was not only a gifted pupil but a member of the university gymnastics team, and Adrienne had had many occasions on which to appreciate the suppleness of her tall, slim body. Obediently, Casey waited for what was to follow. Adrienne spent a moment admiring the way the girl's breasts hung down; two tempting cones of flesh. Her attention was drawn more to the swell of Casey's buttocks, and she traced her fingers along the marks left by the little bikini pants the girl wore when sunbathing.

'You realise what a beautiful target you've left for me,' Adrienne murmured almost lovingly. 'What colour is your bikini, Casey?'

'Blue, Mistress,' Casey replied.

'I think red would suit you better,' Adrienne said decisively. 'Let's find out, shall we?'

With that, she brought her hand down sharply on Casey's waiting backside. She suspected the girl had lot been expecting a slap of such force, as she yelped and made to leap from her perch on Adrienne's lap. Adrienne pressed firmly down in the small of Casey's back, pushing her back into place.

'You're not going anywhere, Casey. Not until this is finished.' Adrienne's hand came down again, harder an before. Casey gave a small protest and wriggled lightly, but made no attempt to move further. She tried accept her punishment mutely, but Adrienne was adept at administering a spanking, and knew exactly where to find the sweet spots that would cause her student most pain. She varied the pace and power of her slaps, so that Casey was never sure when the next one would fall, or where.

True to her word, Adrienne was intent on turning the white flesh on Casey's backside to a deep shade of crimson, and by the time she was satisfied with her work, Casey was sobbing, and begging her tutor not to punish her further. Oblivious to Casey's pleading, Adrienne aimed a couple of slaps at the tops of Casey's thighs, pushing the girl's legs wide apart so that she could attack the sensitive flesh at the crease of her groin.

Despite the pain the spanking was causing Casey, her pussy was still swollen and seeping its feminine juices. Adrienne thrust a finger rudely into Casey's vagina, feeling the ridges of the velvety tube clutch and ripple. Casey whimpered, but this time with pleasure, and she ground her pubic bone against Adrienne's thigh, hoping for satisfaction.

Adrienne smiled and withdrew the finger.

'Please,' Casey entreated her, 'please let me come, Mistress. I've done everything you asked. I've cleaned your shoes. I've brought you off. I've played with myself in the window. Please don't be cruel to me.'

Adrienne sighed. 'Very well.' She toyed at Casey's entrance once more and the girl squirmed, attempting to draw the finger inside herself. Adrienne quickly moved her hand down, and inserted the juice-slick digit into Casey's anus instead. The girl gave a surprised gasp, her sphincter tightening and then relaxing as the finger began to probe more deeply.

'Turn over,' Adrienne ordered, and Casey did as she was told, pivoting to lie face-up on her tutor's knees. Now, Adrienne was able to stare into Casey's eyes as she worked her finger in and out of the girl's arse. She slipped her thumb into Casey's vagina, letting her appreciate the double penetration. Casey moaned and went limp on Adrienne's lap.

'Do you expect me to do all the work?' Adrienne asked sternly. 'Touch your own clit, you lazy girl.'

Without a murmur, Casey did as she was told, rubbing frantically at the little button of flesh. This was the sight Adrienne wished passers-by could appreciate, but she had her reputation to think of. She continued to masturbate Casey in a leisurely fashion, hearing the girl's breathing become ever more ragged as she approached her climax. Casey bucked and writhed, her hips jerking upwards convulsively as her orgasm hit her. She gave a sigh and her hand dropped away from her clit. Adrienne pulled her fingers out of both orifices, and pushed Casey away, letting the girl fall none too gently to the floor.

Suddenly she wanted to be alone.

'Get dressed and get out, Casey,' she said, watching as the girl scrabbled at her clothes, hastily clambering into her knickers and fastening her bra. Once Casey was gone, Adrienne would probably bring herself to another orgasm, thinking about the events that had just taken place – and those which were to come this summer.

Casey paused at the door. 'I'll see you in September,

Mistress,' she said, but she seemed to sense that whatever had happened between herself and her tutor was over. Next term, she would be replaced by another student eager to benefit from Adrienne's extra-curricular teaching.

Adrienne barely noticed Casey as she crept quietly away. Her attention had already turned to Jon Cavendish. In three days she would be meeting him and the rest of his party in New York, and then the adventure would really begin.

Adrienne held up the hand-written sign with Jon Cavendish's name on it, sensing he would spot her without difficulty. There were maybe forty or fifty people waiting to meet passengers from the incoming London flight, but she knew she stood out from the crowd. Her flight from Boston had arrived at Newark airport twenty minutes ahead of schedule, and the London flight had been fifteen minutes late, giving her enough time to negotiate baggage reclaim and even have a cup of coffee in the arrival hall's cafe before meeting the rest of the archaeological party.

A tall, dark-haired man was striding towards her, and she realised that this was the young lecturer. He was in the company of another man, a blond, to whom he bore a striking resemblance, and Adrienne knew this had to be Jonathan's brother, Max. Between them, lugging a heavy-looking holdall, trotted a slightly built girl with fair hair and a pale, English complexion.

'Dr Devaney!' Jonathan's face was all smiles. 'Lovely to meet you at last. Have you been waiting long?'

Adrienne shook her head as they began to walk towards the taxi rank. 'I can always find ways of amusing myself.'

'I'm forgetting myself,' Jonathan said. 'Adrienne, this is my brother, Max, and Justine, one of my star pupils.' There was something in the way he referred to the girl which made Adrienne suspect that Jonathan, like herself, was not averse to furthering teacher-student relationships. Her attention, however, was drawn to Max Cavendish. Both brothers were strikingly handsome, but there was a strangely cruel set to Max's mouth, and his bearing suggested that he enjoyed not only the admiration of others, but also their obedience. Adrienne felt her quim beginning to moisten; though she loved to dominate other women, she also took pleasure in being dominated by a truly masterful man – and she strongly suspected that Max might be such a man. It seemed as though this expedition was to be even more exciting than she had previously suspected.

They were booked into a hotel just off Times Square, in the theatre district of New York. The accommodation was basic, but it was only for two nights, though even that would not have been necessary had the flight they had hoped to take to Montreal not been full. Jonathan and Justine were sharing a room, with Max next door to them, but Adrienne was down a floor, on her own. She glanced round the small, box-like hotel room, which was almost completely filled by a double bed and a pine dressing table. The walls were papered in an insipid floral pattern, the bathtub was of off-white enamel and the shower head dripped persistently. Fourteen floors below her, engines dawdled and horns hooted as the rush hour traffic stood gridlocked. If she had to spend any time in this place awake, she decided, she would go mad.

Sighing, Adrienne touched up her lipstick in the fly-spotted dressing table mirror, grabbed her handbag and went to meet the rest of the party. Max had rung and ordered a table in a small Italian restaurant on the next block, and she was looking forward to the meal. All she had been given on the flight over from Boston had been a packet of pretzels, and that had been a while ago.

She took the lift down to the lobby. The piped Muzak was playing a cheesy rendition of a Diana Ross song she had quite liked until that moment. Jonathan, Max and Justine were already waiting for her. Max had changed out of the jeans he had been wearing into a black jacket, dark blue shirt and stone-coloured chinos, and Adrienne looked him up and down appraisingly. His cool, almost Nordic looks reminded her for one brief moment of her long-dead father. She quickly brushed the thought away. When it came to men, she knew she was no Daddy's girl, simply looking to replace her missing parent; she wanted someone who could play the power game, and she suspected Max was a past master.

Dinner was good enough to take away the dissatisfaction she felt with their accommodation.

Generous plates of fettuccini Alfredo and rich red wine, served by a discreet, unobtrusive waiter, were the perfect backdrop to an animated conversation. Jonathan was eager to discuss their plans for the excavation, but Adrienne could not help noticing that his brother was only paying scant regard to what was being said.

Archaeology bores him, she thought. So why is he here? I know Jon said he needed Max's backing to help get this expedition underway, but anyone else would have paid up and just waited for the results. She thought that perhaps Max was paying a little too much attention to Justine, considering that she was supposed to be his brother's girlfriend, but it seemed that as the evening progressed, she found his keen blue-green gaze turning ever more frequently in her own direction.

When the meal was finally over and Jonathan had settled the bill, Max bent over and whispered to Adrienne, 'When we get back to the hotel, why don't you come up to my room for a little something?'

Adrienne knew there would be no mini-bar in his room, but she sensed he was not offering anything of an alcoholic nature. He fixed her with his direct gaze, and she felt her dark skin colouring slightly. 'Sure. Why not?'

If Jonathan and Justine noticed that Adrienne did not get out of the lift on the floor below theirs, they said nothing. Max wished them goodnight as they fumbled with the key to their room, and pulled Adrienne inside his own. As soon as they were through the door he was kissing her insistently. She responded eagerly, her tongue battling with his as he ran his hands through her long, ringleted hair.

'I know what you want,' he muttered, kneading one of her full breasts through her dress.

'And what's that?' she replied.

'You've had a long term telling all those students of yours what to do. Now you just want to give up all that responsibility and have someone else tell you what to do, isn't that right?'

'You seem pretty sure of yourself,' Adrienne retorted. 'Do you always give instant character analysis?'

'All the time.' Max smiled, loosening his tie. 'I knew Justine was a latent sub as soon as I met her, and I know you wouldn't be averse to the same kind of treatment.'

'And what kind of treatment might that be?' Adrienne asked, feigning innocence.

'This…' Max grabbed her by the wrists, looping his tie around them and knotting it in a makeshift restraint. She was not tightly bound, and Adrienne realised that this was intentional. If Max, for all his sureness, had misjudged her character and she began to protest, he could release her with no real harm done. She knew, however, that she did not want him to release her. Already she could feel her excitement increasing, and she was keen to see just how far he would take her.

He caught hold of her arm and steered her over to the bed. He pushed her on to the paisley-patterned counterpane and she lay there, looking up at him as he turned away and began to hunt through the drawers of his dressing table. 'You have a choice,' he informed her, pulling out another tie and what appeared to be a couple of silk scarves. Did this man travel with his own customised bondage wardrobe? she wondered.

'You can ask me to untie your hands now and leave – or you can stay where you are. But if you stay, you're consenting to let me do whatever I wish to you.'

'Haven't you heard of respecting a girl's limits?' Adrienne snapped back, wondering how much of what he said was a performance for her benefit.

'Of course. I just think your limits might be a little further out than some.' He came to stand by the bed, twining the tie he was holding round and round his hand. 'Admit it, you love this, don't you, Adrienne. You love the idea that you're completely at my mercy.'

Somewhere close by a light flicked on, and Adrienne realised how closely this room was overlooked by those of the hotel that backed on to it. 'Aren't you going to draw the shades?' she asked.

'Don't you like the thought of having an audience?' Max asked, bending close and unfastening her wrists. 'Doesn't it turn you on to think that someone might be watching while I'm spreading you out like this?' As he

49

spoke he wound the tie around her wrist once more, and tethered the free end to one of the bedposts. He repeated the action with her other arm, and she felt her shoulder muscles tauten, grateful that the bed was not particularly wide. He removed her high-heeled shoes and tossed them to the floor, then, without preamble, he reached up her skirt and pulled down her panties, ignoring her wriggling attempts to make that task more difficult. Using the silk scarves, he secured her ankles to the knobs at the foot of the bed, stretching her out like a starfish.

'Should I gag you?' he wondered aloud. 'No, I want to hear you scream my name when you come.'

'You conceited bastard,' Adrienne said, not wanting him to know how turned on she was by the combination of his arrogance and her own vulnerability.

Max said nothing. He sat on the edge of the bed and stroked a possessive hand over the length of her body. She was wearing a soft, plum-coloured polo neck sweater, and he pushed it up her torso, bunching it under her armpits. The bra she wore beneath it was of transparent white nylon, and her large, purplish nipples were completely visible through the material. He ran an experimental finger over the fat buds, which began to swell at his touch. He smirked and pulled open the front-fastening clasp, letting her breasts loll out, large and enticing. She wanted him to play with them, but instead he turned his attention to her leather skirt, raising it so that he could see her sex. She knew she was wet, and she tried to imagine how the darkly pink flesh would look, splayed open to his gaze.

Any other man would have found the sight irresistible but not, it appeared, Max Cavendish. He was on the move again, heading back to the dressing table, and she shivered at what he was holding when he returned. It was a wooden-backed hairbrush with stiff-looking bristles. Adrienne shifted her gaze; the bulge in his chinos was a sizeable one, betraying his apparent indifference to her exposed charms, and she wanted to see him release it.

Instead, he crouched by her, smoothing the bristles of the hairbrush over his palm. 'Are you ready for this?' he asked.

She said nothing, looking at him with mute acquiescence, but she could not prevent a gasp of surprise when he began to scrub at her nipples with the bristles. She felt the tender flesh peaking at the unfamiliar stimulation, and Max smiled at her visible response to his reaction. He applied a little more pleasure, so it began to become painful, but the pain and pleasure were mingling, her nerve-endings transmitting excited little messages down to her womb.

Max ran the brush lightly down over her stomach, and drew it in lazy patterns over her inner thighs. It was more of a tickling sensation now, and almost infuriating. She wriggled in her bonds. 'Ticklish, are we?' he enquired rhetorically, and began to apply the bristles to the soles of her feet.

The constant brushing rapidly became almost unbearable. Max caught hold of one of Adrienne's ankles, devoting his attentions purely to that foot. She twisted and writhed, trying to pull away, and aware that every movement treated him to a view of her pussy from a slightly different angle.

'Please, Max, stop. I can't bear it,' she begged.

'Why should I?' he asked. 'Don't forget, you agreed to this. I might just keep on until you wet yourself with the excitement. How would you like that, Adrienne?'

She said nothing, knowing he would have every intention of carrying out that threat, and that he would take pleasure in witnessing her humiliation. Turning her head away from Max to disguise her shame, she caught sight of what appeared to be a shadowy figure in one of the windows opposite.

'Max, we're being watched, I'm sure we are,' she whispered. She thought back to Casey McGill, standing in the window of her study, frigging herself, and shared some of the girl's embarrassment and arousal at the idea of being seen naked and in the throes of pleasure.

'In that case, let's really give them something to look at,' Max replied. Gripping the hairbrush by its bristles, he moved his hand up so that the wooden handle was between Adrienne's legs. As she watched, he started to tease the entrance to her vagina, first with his fingers and then with the tip of the handle. Adrienne caught her breath as he slowly eased the stubby wooden instrument an inch or so inside her, and began to move it in and out.

She was certain the figure in the window had been joined by a second, and she wondered what emotions were passing through them as they watched a semi-clad black woman being expertly masturbated by a fully dressed white man using a makeshift phallus.

As Max withdrew the hairbrush handle partially, Adrienne could see it was glistening with her juices. She wanted it to be Max's cock which was pumping in and out of her so ruthlessly, emerging slick and wet from her depths, but he had set the rules in this scenario, and she suspected he had no intention of fucking her himself this evening. His finger was on her clit now, describing figures of eight over its sensitive head, and she could no longer devote any rational thought to whatever pleasure he might be deriving from the situation. Her hips jerked, seeking to draw the hairbrush deeper into her muscular sheath, and then she felt her limbs going limp as her orgasm pulled her to the heights before dashing her down again.

She lay panting, a damp sheen on her ebony skin, still clinging to the faint hope that Max might strip off his clothes and take her. However, he was unfastening the ties that bound her to the bed.

Adrienne sat up, rubbing the circulation back into her wrists. Max smiled at her, enigmatically. 'Why don't you take a shower before you go back to your room?' he suggested. 'I'd invite you to stay, but I really do need my sleep.'

Sure, thanks,' she replied, thinking of the unappealing bathtub in her own room. She quickly peeled out of her clothes, feeling no need for modesty after all that had gone before, and slipped into the small bathroom. A blast of hot water on her abused skin and a liberal application of the magnolia-scented body lotion the hotel supplied left her feeling beautifully relaxed.

Her good mood vanished when she stepped back into the bedroom. The clothes she had left scattered on Max's bed were nowhere to be seen.

'Max, is this some kind of joke?' she asked, feeling unaccountably irritated.

'Sorry, darling, I forgot to tell you the game wasn't quite over,' Max replied languidly. 'You'll get them back tomorrow. But now I'm going to have to ask you to leave.'

Adrienne glanced down at her naked body. 'I can't go out there like this!'

'Of course not. Here, take this.' Max pressed her clutch bag and a hand towel into her grasp, before steering her firmly out into the corridor and slamming the door shut behind her. She hammered on it for a few seconds, shouting to him to open it and stop being such a bastard, then started at the sound of footsteps on the thin pile carpet.

She wrapped herself in the towel as best she could. It was only big enough to cover part of her breasts and her belly, leaving her bottom completely exposed. She pressed her back against the wall as an elderly couple walked towards her. They regarded her quizzically, and she said, 'I'm locked out of my room.'

'Need any help, honey?' the old woman asked.

Adrienne shook her head. 'No, I'm fine thanks.' She was aware that the towel was slipping, and that at any second she would treat the couple to a sight of her large, dark nipples.

'Okay, if you're sure...'

They began to shuffle off down the corridor, seeming to take an awful long time to reach their own room. Adrienne knew she could not risk using the elevator, and would have to return to the floor below using the stairs. Hastily she padded in search of the stairwell, afraid that at any moment she would be spotted by another guest. She almost ran down the flight of stairs, and opened the door onto her floor to find herself confronted by a teenage boy clutching a bucket full of ice and a couple of vending machine packets of pretzels. He leered at her, and she fled before he could say anything, aware that he would have a good view of her naked buttocks as she retreated to her room.

At least Max had given her her bag, which meant she had her key. If she had had to go down to the lobby and ask for help, she would have died of shame. She fumbled with the bag and found her key. As she did so the towel fell away completely from her body, but she was past caring who might see her.

Adrienne collapsed on to the bed, cursing Max Cavendish and yet aware that he seemed to know exactly how to turn her on. Everything he did had been designed to humiliate and shame her, and yet her pussy still throbbed with a deep sexual excitement. She knew he had in no way fulfilled his promise to take her to her limits, but perhaps on Odinland she would have the chance to find out just how far Max was prepared to go.

Chapter Four

The small plane skittered over the waves, coming close to the rocky shore of the island that was known as Odinland. Its passengers craned their necks to see out of the window, eager for a first glimpse of their destination. The flight from Newfoundland had been a rough one, with turbulent winds buffeting the little craft, and all four were anxious to touch down on firm ground once more.

Max glanced across the cramped cabin to where Justine was sitting. The headphones of a personal stereo were plugged into her ears, and she had been steadfastly ignoring him throughout the journey. They had hardly spoken since leaving England, and her silence frustrated him. He wanted desperately to know how she felt towards him. As far as he was aware, she had said nothing about the incident in his playroom to Jonathan; it was better all round if his brother remained innocent of that little encounter. Max had made the mistake of boasting about his conquest of Jonathan's previous girlfriend, Vicky, and had received a black eye and cracked ribs from his brother for his pains. And once the plane deposited them on the island, the four explorers would see no other living soul for ten days; it was time enough for tensions to build to an unbearable level if a wrong word was said or an old hurt brought to the surface.

The plane began its descent, its landing place a long stretch of greyish sand, evidence of the island's volcanic origins. Its pilot, a stocky, red-haired man in his early forties who went by the name of Bud, announced, 'Okay, guys, make sure you're strapped in real tight. It looks like we're in for a bumpy landing.'

This was no exaggeration. The ground seemed to loom up with sickening speed as Bud fought to keep control of the aircraft. One wheel touched down and the plane juddered across the beach. Adrienne caught hold of Max's arm, her expression fearful. Justine's face was buried in her hands. Cargo thumped against the walls of the small hold. Only Jonathan seemed relatively calm, and Max had the sudden conviction that, following his near-death experience in the Amazon jungle, his brother believed himself immune to harm.

The second wheel hit the soft sand as the plane began to slow, the engines whining in protest. It was a relief to everyone on board when the aircraft finally came to a halt and they could unbuckle their seat belts.

Outside, there was a strong breeze blowing, taking he heat off the July day. They stood on the deserted beach, looking around at the flat grey sand and the choppy grey sea. Columns of rock stood a little way off the shoreline, pitted and eroded by centuries of tidal movement, reaching skywards like despairing fingers. Gulls wheeled and swooped, occasionally diving down to pluck a fish from the water, their cries echoing like those of the damned. It felt to Max as though they had come to the end of the world.

'So I'll see you in ten days' time,' Bud was saying as he shook hands with Jonathan. 'Don't you all go getting up to mischief, now. I mean, hell, you could really live it up in a place like this.'

He climbed back into the cockpit and started the engine.

As soon as he had gone they would be alone. Their only contact with civilisation would be a two-way radio which was stowed in their luggage. If anything went wrong they would need it to summon help. But nothing is going to go wrong, Max told himself as the plane began to rise into the sky, rapidly becoming nothing more than a dark speck against the low clouds. We're just going to dig up the remains of a group of dead Vikings who've apparently been erased from history for performing acts too unspeakable to contemplate. What could be simpler than that?

They set up camp in a sheltered cove on the south side of the island, about a mile's walk along the beach from where Bud had deposited them. Having studied the only available writings on the Odinland settlement, which were frustratingly sketchy, Jonathan was convinced that this was the place where the islanders had built their village. Max was not convinced; from what he had seen, this stretch of the coastline was made up of a series of practically identical little inlets. This was not a welcoming place, despite Jonathan's tales about the fertile land and the pleasant climate, and he could not understand why the settlers had chosen to land here. There must have been other islands where the sea did not suck and churn around the rocky outcrops with such ferocity, and where there was not the all-pervading sense that, somehow, they were being watched. He bit his lip and said nothing; after all, it had taken him a while to get used to the quiet Suffolk countryside after the bustle of London. Two nights ago they had been in New York, the city that never slept, and Max told himself that his paranoia was the natural reaction of any town dweller when confronted with total isolation.

With all four of them working in harmony it did not take long to pitch their tents. Max was sharing with Adrienne, and he stacked up his rucksack full of clothes and odds and ends and his sleeping-bag at one end of the tent.

'I shouldn't have thought you were used to roughing it like this,' Adrienne said as she watched him sort through his possessions.

'There's a lot you don't know about me,' he replied. 'Jon and I used to go camping every summer when we were in the Scouts. I used to hate it, but it's where I learned my facility with knots, so it wasn't an entirely wasted experience.'

'I'm pleased to hear it,' Adrienne murmured. 'But stop reminiscing about your misspent youth. We've got work to get on with.'

Jonathan was standing outside the tents, clutching a ball of plasticised twine. 'We're going to mark off the area first,' he explained to Max. 'That way we can catalogue the findings more easily. I don't think we're going to have to dig too far down; after all, there was only ever one settlement on the island and nothing was ever built on top of it. Normally, the past comes in layers, and you have to dig down through the detritus of the past few centuries to find what you're looking for. Here we don't have that problem.'

'Great,' Max said. 'So let's get down to it.'

It took three-quarters of an hour for the novelty of the excavation to wear off as far as Max was concerned. Jonathan had warned him that it would be painstaking work, but if it took the little archaeological team this long merely to section off the ground, how long would it take for them to actually get round to digging? He had been mad to agree to ten days of this, when he could have been trawling the scene back in England, looking for someone to replace Anita in his life. Still, there was always the prospect of another session with the inventive Dr Devaney to while away the long nights. He pictured her as she had looked when he had thrown her out of his hotel room, her enticing dark body only minimally covered by the tiny white towel, and he regretted not having given her luscious bottom the spanking for which it cried out. He had thought seriously about inviting her back to his room the following evening. She had been eager to feel more than the handle of his hairbrush inside her, and he would have happily complied, had there not been something holding him back.

The truth was that Adrienne, for all her charms, was only a distraction. The real prize, the Grail that drew him on the way the thought of retrieving old bones drew Jonathan on, was the ultimate submission of Justine McClure to his desires. She was ripe for plucking; she had proved that the moment she had agreed to let him snap those cuffs round her wrists. If that stupid cow Anita hadn't poked her nose in he could have had Justine by now: felt himself penetrate the depths of her warm, wet mouth; her silky quim; her tight arsehole ...

Thoughts like that were futile distractions, causing his cock to swell uncomfortably against the confines of his black jeans. Though she was working only a few feet from him, he knew that Justine was, mentally, an unbridgeable distance away, her head full of an imagined Viking settlement long since dead and buried.

'Does anyone mind if I go for a walk?' he asked. 'I'd like to take a look around the island, see what I can find.'

'Sure, go ahead,' Adrienne muttered, glancing up from the reel of twine she was unwinding. 'We'll manage without you for a while, won't we, Jon?'

'Uh – what? Oh, yes,' Jonathan replied, distractedly. 'We won't really need you till we start digging, Max.'

Max glanced at his watch. 'Right, well, I'll see you in, say, an hour?' he said, assuming that by the time he returned the others would be ready for food. He didn't mind helping prepare meals; he was just bored out of his skull by the tedious job of mapping the ground.

He noticed Justine glance up briefly as he walked past her, and he winked casually. She blushed furiously and returned to her work. Now, what could have brought that on? he wondered to himself. Unless she's thinking about me, the way I'm thinking about her.

The thought lightened his step as he began to make his way up the small incline that led away from the campsite. Perhaps he should have suggested that she join him on his wanderings; if he could only get her from under Jonathan's nose for long enough, he could introduce her to the joys of a decent spanking. He wanted to see her little bottom turn red under his palm, and began to imagine how she would react. Would she try to bear the blows in silence, or would she yelp and squeal? Would she wriggle away from his palm? Would she cry, and beg him to stop? And then, when the stinging pain began to change to a deeper pleasure, would she beg him to carry on?

He smiled to himself as he strolled along the soft, springy grass. There was the beginning of a small wood to his left, but he decided against exploring it. Something about this island was definitely making him feel uneasy, though he could not have put his anxiety into words. He was only aware of a vague prickling at the nape of his neck, and a desire to keep a distance between himself and the dark, almost forbidding clump of pine trees. Stories Jonathan had told him were buzzing in the back of his brain; there was at least one archaeological dig his brother knew of which had come to grief because the locals had warned them not to unearth a burial site. Max suspected the problems had been caused by the superstitious peasants, rather than their vengeful ancestors, but he could not help thinking about the accidents and strange illnesses which had befallen those who had unearthed Tutankhamen's tomb. Telling himself not to be such an idiot, he trudged on up the hill.

At the top of the rise he stopped and looked behind him. The path he had taken must have wound its way around the side of the hill without his being aware of it, for the little camp was hidden from his view by the thick knot of pines. In front of him the land sloped away into a shallow valley, and beyond that the landscape rose once more and became mountainous, the rocks striated in deep hues of red and ochre.

Max's eyes were drawn to the foot of the valley. Almost directly below him, set into the sandy earth, was a thick wooden pole, from which short lengths of chain were hanging. Obviously a Viking artefact of some description, left behind when the village was abandoned. He was about to turn back and tell Jonathan that they were about to start digging in the wrong place, when a thought struck him.

How could that pole still be standing after a thousand years?

Something is wrong here, Max told himself. Wood rots. Trees can live for hundreds of years, but wood that's been cut down starts to decay. And those chains don't look at all rusty. Which means whoever put that pole there did so fairly recently.

As he tried to make sense of what he was seeing, his eye was caught by movement on the other side of the valley. He looked, and looked again, hardly believing what he was seeing. Three people were making their way cautiously down a rocky path to the valley floor; two men, with a woman between them. The woman seemed to be slowing the progress of the other two, and Max realised they were having to guide her, as her wrists appeared to be chained together behind her back.

He dropped to the grass, afraid they might have seen him, but none of the three was looking in his direction. As they headed for the pole he studied them more closely. The men had fair hair, woven into plaits that reached easily to their pectoral muscles, and the woman was a redhead. The long, flame-coloured fall of her hair reminded Max irresistibly of Anita, and he watched as she stumbled and almost tripped. The taller of the men said something, prodded her in the ribs, and laughed. She glowered at her tormentor, but did not reply.

When they reached the pole, they halted. The tall man began to speak again. Max had no idea what was being said, but the tone was reminiscent of a magistrate's summing-up at the end of a trial. The man seemed to be making points, and after every point his shorter, stocky companion would nod. The woman's eyes were downcast, but occasionally she would glance up, obviously protesting at something that had been said. Eventually, the tall man paused, apparently waiting for the other to agree to his proposal. The shorter man nodded, and began to unlock the woman's chains.

As soon as her hands were free, the two men grasped

hold of her and began to systematically strip her. She did not protest, seeming almost resigned to her fate. She wore a long, rust-coloured woollen dress which fell in pleated folds to the middle of her calves, and beneath that strips of cloth were wrapped around her breasts and loins in lieu of underwear. It did not take long to relieve her of these items, and Max was given a good view of her pale body. She was slim, with the look of a woman whose body was kept in trim by hard, physical work, but her breasts were large, and set high on her chest, topped with shell-pink nipples. Her belly was flat, and her hips flared out from a small waist. Unable to resist glancing down between her legs, Max was surprised to see that her sex was smoothly shaven.

She was turned to face the wooden pole, and now Max realised that the chains that hung there finished in thick iron cuffs. The woman was made to raise her arms above her head and cross them at the wrists, then the cuffs were fastened securely in place. At another order, she spread her legs shoulder width apart, the movement separating the high, round cheeks of her backside.

Max was not surprised to feel the beginning of an erection stirring in his boxer shorts. No man could have remained immune to the sight of such a beautiful woman being stripped and put into restraints; he hoped they did not intend to simply leave her there, but that a punishment was to be administered.

The taller man's next movement raised Max's hopes further. He reached down and uncoiled something from his belt. That something was a whip, made of thin, plaited leather strips attached to a handle of some blackish wood. The girl was watching him flex it over her shoulder, and she shuddered as he experimentally flicked the air.

The second man began to stroke his hands along the length of the girl's tethered body, exhibiting a strange pride in the lean lines of her belly and haunches. It was almost as though he was showing off a prize mare, or a sleek racing car of which he was exceptionally fond. Max had originally assumed that this was the girl's husband, or her lover, but now he was beginning to realise the man was actually her owner.

It seemed inevitable that he would pause when his hands reached her buttocks, and bring his palm down on the taut flesh with a stinging slap. The girl flinched, even though Max suspected she had been expecting the blow. Her two chastisers laughed, and her master applied the flat of his hand to her other cheek with equal force.

Max raised himself to a sitting position and began to amble with the fly of his jeans. His erection was pressing against the denim and causing him some discomfort. It made sense to free it and, once it was free, to begin to stroke his loosely curled fingers up and own its length. After all, he was safe enough up here, and unlikely to be disturbed. His only regret was that he could not witness the girl's punishment from closer quarters; he could imagine without difficulty how the man's hands would have left a flaming imprint on her buttocks, but he would have loved to see it for himself, and feel the heat of her abused flesh.

The stocky man stepped back, and aimed a slap at each of the girl's inner thighs. The flesh there would be softer, less used to being beaten, and her response was vocal. She was pleading with her master; Max suspected she was promising to behave, to do anything he required of her, as long as he did not hit her again. The pleas and promises were ignored as the man applied the flat of his hand liberally to her backside.

At last he stepped back, pleased with his handiwork. He nodded to his companion, urging him forward to begin his own part of the girl's punishment. Max sighed, resisting the temptation to let his hand speed its movement along his rigid shaft. Drops of clear, salty juice were slowly oozing from the tip of his glans as his excitement mounted.

The girl's skin would be sore, sensitised by the thorough spanking it had just received. She would feel every lash of the whip the taller man was flexing more intensely, pain mounting on pain. In the hands of a skilful master, Max knew that pain would meld with the endorphin rush of orgasm; he had witnessed the sight many times. He wanted to see the redhead shake and whimper under the force of the whip, but he needed to see her agony transformed to ecstasy.

The man was delaying the moment when he would bring the whip arcing down onto her reddened buttocks, and the girl was obviously agitated, shifting from foot to foot. A barked order stilled her movements and she stood passively, waiting. There was the faintest whistling sound as the leather whip slashed through the air, and then a crack as it landed on her right arse cheek. She stifled a cry and shook in her chains, but she seemed determined not to give the two men the satisfaction of seeing how much the stroke had pained her. Perhaps she sensed she had already humiliated herself enough by begging to be spared her punishment.

A second stroke fell, on the left buttock this time, and again the girl remained stoically calm. This seemed to infuriate the tall man; he angled the next so that it curled slightly around her body, the thicker part of the lash landing on her buttock but the thinner tip catching her on the hip bone. This did hurt, and she yelped. Smiling, he repeated the stroke on her opposite hip, the weal crossing over one he had already raised. He paused, as though considering his options. The girl's head was drooping, and her master caught a fistful of her long red hair and raised her eyes to meet his.

The tall man gave a flick of his wrist, and the whip streaked across the tops of the girl's thighs. Skilfully, he laid a second stroke just a little higher, just below the underhang of her buttocks. Max, now masturbating at a more furious pace, had to admit the man was a master of his trade; every stroke of the whip seemed designed to cause pain without undue damage, perhaps because the girl would be expected to return to whatever menial work was required of her once the punishment was finished.

The girl was sobbing openly now, but it seemed the tall man had one last trick up his sleeve. This time, when he cracked the whip, it was aimed squarely at the crown of her left breast. As the girl's back was to Max, he could not see the blow land, but the girl's reaction proved how much it had stung, as she writhed convulsively in her chains. Max knew before the next stroke fell that its target would be her left breast, and he was not disappointed. He shuddered, and his grip on his cock tightened.

The two men chattered excitedly amongst themselves as they unfastened the girl's wrist cuffs. She did not resist as her master pushed her onto all fours, and fumbled with his woollen breeches. They dropped to his knees and he grasped his short, stubby penis, which already stood stiffly to attention. Kneeling behind the girl, he shoved his cock without preamble into her sex; the ease with which it appeared to slide into her testified that the punishment had excited her as much as it had pained her. Her master grasped her firmly by the hips, and continued to push into her until his loins pressed against her recently whipped buttocks. Max knew the man could not have chosen a better position in which to take her; she was guaranteed to feel him slamming into her sore flesh with every thrust.

The second man stood in front of her, and he, too, released his cock from the confines of his trousers. It was longer than that of his companion, though not so thick, and he waved it in the face of the slave girl, wiping its head along her lips until she took it obediently into her mouth. As her master thrust into her from behind, he jolted her towards the man in front, so that her mouth bobbed up and down on his proffered shaft. Her body was drenched with sweat now, and her hair was matted around her face, but she was still a magnificent sight to Max's eyes as the two men took her from each end.

The tall man was the first to come, pulling out of her mouth to let his seed slide down her chin and onto her heavy, hanging breasts. He grabbed a hank of her hair, and used it to wipe his cock clean before stuffing it back into his breeches. Behind her, her master was pumping more furiously, obviously close to orgasm himself. With a groan that was audible the length of the valley, he gave one last frantic thrust, and came deep inside her.

She slumped on her haunches as he withdrew from her juicy channel, her body heaving and exhausted, but the men were not finished with her.

At a command from her master, she reached between her legs and began to rub herself, her fingers a blur as she was ordered to bring herself to the orgasm their combined exertions had not wrung from her.

It was the sight of the girl, kneeling in the dirt, bringing herself to climax, which finally caused the semen to rise up Max's shaft and burst from his glans, pumping rhythmically down over his wrist.

He must have slept for a few minutes, for when he next opened his eyes and looked down to the valley floor the two men and their slave had disappeared. If it had not been for the scuffed-up earth around the wooden pole, Max could quite easily have believed that the whole thing had been a dream brought on by the heat of the afternoon and his desire to punish Justine.

As he cleaned his now-flaccid penis and adjusted his clothing, the significance of what he had just seen finally hit him. His creeping fear that something was amiss on Odinland had been justified. The island was not deserted, after all. There were at least three people here, people who believed in a society that saw nothing wrong with keeping a woman as a slave and punishing her for any misdemeanours. And if there were three of them, there were undoubtedly more. He had to let Jonathan and the others know what had happened.

His descent of the hill was scrambled, his booted feet hurrying down the rocky path back to the camp. Adrienne straightened her back and looked up at his approach.

'Hey, Max, slow down,' she called.

'Jon! Jon!' Max exclaimed. 'You're never going to believe what I've seen. Come with me. It's…'

He grabbed Jonathan's arm excitedly, but his brother brushed his hand away. Max noticed there was a strange, anguished expression on Jonathan's face. 'We've got no time to go anywhere,' the younger man said. 'It's Justine. She – she's disappeared.'

Chapter Five

She had only wanted a bar of chocolate. Sometimes Justine cursed her fast metabolism; while it meant she was not prone to putting on weight, it left her craving food after any prolonged period of hard, physical work. After an hour or so of fetching and carrying for Jonathan and Dr Devaney, she could feel herself becoming tetchy and irritable, needing a fix of something sugary and calorie-laden to soothe her hunger pangs and give her enough energy to last until whenever Max returned and he others decided to break for food.

In the inside pocket of her rucksack was a stash of chocolate bars, which she had bought in an all-night deli in New York: Mars Bars, Snickers, Baby Ruths and a big bag of peanut butter cups, her all-time favourite. Slipping away to the campsite, she had wormed her way into the tent she was sharing with Jonathan in search of that rucksack. It would not hurt to take five minutes away from the dig, she had told herself, not after Jonathan had let his brother go wandering, when the man's physical strength would have helped them finish the job that much sooner. Intent on what she was doing, she did not hear the near-silent tread of footsteps on the hard earth outside the tent. Her fingers were just closing around a Hershey Bar when a big hand clamped itself across her mouth. Unable to scream, she at least had the presence of mind to kick back, her booted foot making connection with a solid shin. The grip on her face loosened only slightly as she wriggled, trying to break away from whoever it was who held her. Adrenalin coursed through her body, making her heart pound frantically in her chest.

Terror overtook her as she realised the strength of her unknown assailant. Hard as she tried to free herself, he was too powerful to fight against. He began to haul her backwards out of the tent, her limbs flailing as she tried to resist. She had time only to register the calluses on the hand that covered her palm, and the scent he exuded, a mixture of fresh sweat and a more earthy masculinity, and then her head cracked hard against the central tent pole and she knew nothing but blackness.

She came to and saw a face staring at her. A headache throbbed low at the back of her skull, and when she tried to pull away from the man standing before her, she could not move. Glancing around, she realised that her arms and legs were securely tethered to two freestanding poles in the middle of a circle of earth.

'Who are you?' she asked, her voice trembling with fear. 'What the hell are you playing at?'

The man gazed at her, saying nothing.

'Don't just ignore me,' she demanded. 'Untie me. Let me go.'

Again he stared at her, a look of blank incomprehension on his face as he followed the movements of her mouth, and she had the sudden, unsettling realisation that he could not speak English. She looked at him, properly this time. He was bending, so his face was level with hers; if he straightened up, she decided, he would probably be taller than either Jonathan or Max, both of whom stood six foot in height. And he was not only tall, but broad; wide-shouldered and sturdy, with hands whose dimensions she had become all too familiar with as he had tried to heave her out of the tent. His hair was his glory; a thick, wild strawberry blond mane that fell well beyond his shoulders in loose waves, with two small plaits in the front section, one on each side of his head. His eyes were grey and his face young and unlined. He dressed strangely, too: a loose tunic of coarsely woven fabric, and dun-coloured breeches that were bound up to his knees with criss-crossing straps of leather. He looks like something out of the books I had when I was a kid, Justine thought crazily. He's a storybook Viking.

This was stupid. There were no such things as Vikings, not any more. They had mutated from the wild adventurers who had raped and pillaged their way across half the world into city-suited Danes and Norwegians more familiar with corporate raiding than its physical counterpart. And even if the Norsemen did still exist, it would not be here on Odinland, an island deserted and forgotten about for the best part of a thousand years. She had merely banged her head crawling around in the cramped confines of that lousy tent, and this whole thing was a concussion-induced dream.

Though if that were the case, surely she would be able to walk away from the situation. As she struggled to find even an inch of purchase in the unforgiving ropes that circled her wrists and ankles, she knew with a horrifying certainty that she was not hallucinating: she really was tied up. Suddenly, Justine felt very alone and very vulnerable.

If she knew how far from the base camp she had been taken, she could have risked a scream. Jonathan and Adrienne would have been able to hear her; if not, perhaps she might even have attracted the attention of the errant Max. Though what he would say if he saw her bound and immobile did not bear thinking about. She could still remember the firm, insistent pressure of his hands as he had kneaded her breasts while she hung in willing suspension in his playroom. She thought of the moments before Anita had made her unexpected entrance, when she had felt those hands sliding lower, unbuckling the belt of her jeans, and pushing aside the loose denim to fondle her sex through the thin cotton of her panties before bringing her to a shattering orgasm. It shamed her to admit, even to herself, that for all her protestations, whatever he had done to her, she had made only a token resistance.

She shuddered, feeling a steady pulse beginning to beat between her legs. Bloody Max Cavendish: why did the thought of him turn her on so much, when he was the cold, cruel opposite of his kind-hearted brother? Justine longed to rub her thighs together to soothe the dull ache, but her abductor had secured her legs too widely apart, and she wriggled in a mixture of alarm and frustration.

If she could not summon help, this man could do anything to her. He came close, ruffling her soft, fair hair and stroking her cheek. She tried not to flinch at his touch, not wanting him to know how frightened she was, and his big, work-worn hand slowly moved down her neck. Justine had always liked to be caressed there, and she could not prevent a small sigh of pleasure as his fingers circled over the sensitive flesh below her jaw line.

Any pleasure vanished completely at his next movement. He grabbed at her faded red tee-shirt and pulled it out of the waistband of her jeans. With almost no visible effort he ripped the tee-shirt in half, shredding it from her body and tossing it to the ground. A puzzled frown crossed his face and she followed his gaze down her own torso, to realise he was staring at the lacy bra she was wearing. He reached out a curious finger and touched the soft material of one cup, then pulled experimentally at the shoulder strap. If he expected the elasticated strap to tear as easily as the tee-shirt had done, he was disappointed, and Justine winced as he tugged harder. After a moment's hesitation he bent and pulled a small knife from the strapping around his knee. Justine watched the blade glittering in the sunlight before he began to saw at her bra straps. That done, he cut the strip of fabric that separated the cups, letting the now useless garment fall to the floor as he sheathed the knife once more.

Justine felt cool air on her small, pale breasts. She was aware that her nipples were stiffening, though she could not have said whether it was the breeze that caused them to harden, or her own sense of fear, mingled with anticipation. Part of her mind was thousands of miles away from this forest clearing, back in a room in a Suffolk farmhouse, where the man who gazed on her semi-naked body, liking what he saw, was Max.

Hands closed around her breasts, cupping and squeezing them roughly. She wriggled in her bonds; wanting to pull away and yet, despite herself, feeling a moistening in her quim and the seam of her jeans beginning to chafe against her swelling labia.

'Stop it, you're hurting me,' she whimpered, as the man continued to toy with her nipples, pinching them hard between his finger and thumb till small, dull fires of pain raged within them. It was useless to protest: this man, whoever he was, could not understand a word she said, and she suspected that even if he could, he would still have paid no attention to her pleading. And yet, as she rode the pain, it was beginning to turn to a new sensation – one that, had she cared to put a name to it, she would have described as pleasure.

As he turned his attention to her jeans, she noticed that the creamy flesh of her breasts was mottled with the purplish-red marks his powerful fingers had left. Despite the roughness of his touch, she was already beginning to miss it as he fumbled with her belt. That, and the fly buttons of her jeans, presented no problem to him and without ceremony he yanked both her jeans and panties down to her knees, hobbling her further.

For a moment he contemplated the twin globes of her naked backside. Then he used his big hands to pull her cheeks apart. She could not see his face, but could imagine him gazing intently at the dark furrow his actions had revealed. He loosed his grip and, with shocking suddenness, his hand smacked down hard on each one in turn, her flesh stinging and reddening under the force of the blows. He smiled and muttered something in satisfaction, before peppering her buttocks with further slaps. Justine wriggled in her bonds, trying to jerk her body away from his punishing palm, but he caught his hand in her fair hair and pulled her closer to him. She yelped and whimpered as the skin of her arse turned a fiery red, conscious that even as she registered the stinging pain, her pussy continued to throb and demand relief.

He thrust his hand between her legs, encountering the wetness of her quim, and she moaned. First one, then a second finger was pushed roughly into the entrance of her cunt, stretching her wide. She could not stop him from exploring every inch of her, and in truth she could not have said she wanted to. Max was right: it did turn her on to be tied up, helpless, unable to prevent herself from being taken. A third finger was added to the two which probed her, as her juices began to flow copiously. He scooped up her honeyed lubrication and smeared it over her clit, rubbing at the hard little button till she was half-delirious with ecstasy. This man knew what he was doing: he wanted to give her pleasure, as well as take his own.

And then the finger dabbled in her wetness again, but this time it rubbed at the opening of her other, forbidden hole. No one had touched Justine there before, and she gasped as the finger slowly wormed its way inside her. She felt herself submit to the intrusive digit, and her captor gave a grunt of satisfaction as he watched her writhe, impaled on his strong, thick fingers, driving herself on towards orgasm.

Suddenly he pulled out, leaving Justine flushed and panting for breath. She watched silently as he dropped his own breeches, gazing wide-eyed at the thickness of his erect cock. Until then she had always thought of Jonathan as well endowed, and she suspected, from the size of the bulge she had seen in Max's trousers when he had been playing with her back at his home, that the elder of the Cavendish brothers was similarly blessed. But nothing she had previously experienced compared to the hard column of flesh that jutted upwards from the nest of gingery-blond hair at this Viking's groin. She yearned to reach out and stroke it, to fall to her knees and take it into her mouth.

He seemed to sense what she was thinking, for he grinned proudly and began to stroke the length of his shaft, pulling the foreskin away from the bulbous glans that was already weeping tears of excitement. Justine could not tear her eyes away from the movement of his fingers.

Her sex felt cavernous and empty, and all she could imagine was that huge cock plunging into it and filling it utterly.

When he came behind her again and grasped her firmly around the waist, she was ready for him. She had never before felt so wet, her sticky juices trickling down her thighs. The blunt head of his erection bumped against the entrance to her vagina, and she mewled and thrust her hips backwards, seeking to draw him inside.

And then she felt him move slightly, so that now he was lodged against her anus. This she had not expected, and she tried to pull away, but his grip was too strong. His cock-head thrust at her, insistently seeking entry. Justine bowed her head, acquiescing to the inevitable.

He reached out and grasped one of her nipples, pinching it hard between thumb and forefinger. Her attention briefly diverted, she was drawn back to herself as she felt his cock penetrate her in one sudden, fierce thrust.

She would never have thought it was possible to take something of those dimensions but, somehow, he was working deeper into her, stretching the virgin walls of her anus. He was moving slowly, attempting to accustom her to the length and girth of the member that she gripped so tightly within, and she was about to thank him inwardly, until he began to thrust, causing her to cry out. Now he was more urgent, muttering something guttural in her ear which could have been a compliment or a curse. She felt the coarse fabric of his shirt scratching against her back, and heard the slap of his heavy balls against her sore buttocks as he buried himself in her as deeply as he could go. Tethered as she was, she was compelled to move with him, trying to accustom herself to the strange new sexual sensations that were building within her.

His hand was clamped against the gentle curve of her stomach, manoeuvring her into a position where he could reach down and rub her clit. The searing pain his initial thrusts had caused was dampened down by the pressure of his fingers against her pleasure bud, and despite herself, she felt the orgasmic sensations beginning to mount once more. This time he showed no inclination to withdraw as her climax approached. Gasping and groaning, Justine forgot the humiliating, undignified position he had placed her in, and surrendered to the fierce, heavy waves that pounded through her. Blood sang in her ears, and for a moment she thought she would lose consciousness. The muscles of her sphincter fluttered around the solid length of flesh that was embedded in her anus, and she felt her Viking lover grow briefly larger and harder, before his body began to jerk and he came, shooting his creamy seed deep inside her.

Abruptly, he let go, leaving her to dangle in her bonds like a broken marionette as she attempted to regain her breath. Her rational mind was struggling to comprehend what had happened to her, incredulous that she could have wrung any enjoyment from it. And yet the orgasm he had induced had been the most powerful she had ever experienced: Jonathan, for all his tender lovemaking and his knowledge of what made her come, had never solicited its equal.

She glanced up from beneath her sweat-soaked fringe, watching as her captor casually adjusted his clothing. For a moment she thought he would leave her where she was tied, but he pulled the little knife from his knee-strap, and used it to sever her bonds.

'Thanks,' she muttered, stepping away from the wooden poles and pulling up her jeans and panties, briefly aware of the cooling stickiness between the cheeks of her bottom. She attempted to rub the life back into her aching wrists. However, before she could do so, he had grabbed both her hands in one of his own and tied them together with a length of rope that, she realised, was long enough for him to grasp and leave about a foot of space between them.

The jerk of his head was unmistakable. He wanted her to follow him, and she had no choice but to do as he wished. She stumbled after him as he walked confidently out of the clearing, her hands tied before her and the sweat of their sexual exertions drying on her partially clad body. As he led her to some unknown destination, she wondered for a moment whether Jonathan and Adrienne had missed her, and whether they would have any idea where to begin looking for her if they had.

'I tell you,' Jonathan said, 'one minute she was here, and the next she'd vanished. I don't understand where she could have gone.'

'I thought perhaps she was unwell, and had gone back to the tent to lie down,' Adrienne added. 'But when I came looking I couldn't find her anywhere.'

'It's not like her, Max,' Jonathan persisted. He sat down heavily, oblivious to the damp earth that stained his work-worn jeans. 'She's been on digs before. She's one of the most conscientious girls I've ever worked with. She wouldn't just slope off without telling me. I mean, it's not as if there's anywhere for her to go. This whole island is dead.'

'That's where you're wrong, I'm afraid,' Max said.

'What are you talking about?' Jonathan asked.

'This is what I was trying to tell you. This island. It

isn't deserted.'

'Max, have you got sunstroke?' Jonathan's expression was one of blatant disbelief. 'How can this place not be deserted? No one's lived here for a thousand years, and there's been no other archaeological exploration planned here. I would have known about it if there had been.'

'Jon, there are people here. I've seen them.' Max thought back to the erotic spectacle he had witnessed so recently, and despite the gravity of the situation, his cock began to rise under the influence of this mental stimulation. 'I know you're going to think I'm talking a load of bollocks, but I saw three people in a valley not two miles away from here. There were two men, and they had a woman tied up and they both fucked her.'

'Max, you're thinking with your balls again,' Jonathan scoffed. 'I know what you're like if you don't have sex for a while. You fell asleep, and you dreamed it all. You'll be telling me they were Vikings next.'

'Would you believe that's exactly what they were?'

'Maybe you were right, Jon,' Adrienne butted in.

'Maybe we shouldn't have brought him with us, money or no money.'

'Look, I'm telling you. I was there. I saw it.' There was a low edge of exasperation in Max's voice. 'I don't care whether you believe me or not. There are people on this island, and they may have taken Justine.'

'Taken her?' Jonathan leaped to his feet.

'It's a possibility. Why don't we go back and look at the tent again?'

The three of them dashed over to the little tent that Justine and Jonathan were sharing. Jonathan poked his lead through the flap. 'It does look like something's gone on in here, I have to admit. The contents of Justine's rucksack are all over the floor. Didn't that make you think something was wrong, Adrienne?'

'I just thought she was a little on the messy side,' she admitted. 'Don't forget, I don't know her the way you obviously do.'

'That's neither here nor there,' Max said, anxious to defuse any squabbling before it began. 'Look at the way the dirt's all scuffed up at the entrance to the tent. I hate to say this, but it looks like there's been a struggle. God, for all that you two are supposed to be good at digging evidence out of the earth, you haven't half been blind here.'

Adrienne seemed about to rise to his criticism, but Jonathan's next words stilled her. 'I've found footprints,' he said. 'The earth's too dusty here for me to able to make them out clearly, but it looks like there's one set, and…' he paused, his face anguished '…whoever they belong to was dragging something.'

'Come on,' Max said. 'Let's see where they lead.'

He set off away from the campsite at a fast pace, Jonathan and Adrienne following behind him. The footsteps wound their way up a dirt track between the trees. As the earth grew softer where it was shaded by overhanging foliage, it became easier to see that they were indeed tracking the marks left by a large pair of feet, and what appeared to be two boot heels working a small, shallow groove in the damp ground.

In any other circumstances this might have been a pleasant walk: the trees cast a cooling green shade, and birds called to each other from high in the branches. However, all three were too preoccupied by their thoughts to pay much attention to their surroundings. After about fifteen minutes of walking, the densely-spaced trees began to thin out, and the trail of footsteps came to a halt in what could loosely be called a clearing, but was in truth little more than a circle of earth tramped down in the middle of the forest.

Max's eyes took in the two sturdy wooden poles, set about five feet apart, and the muddle of footprints that surrounded them.

'Well, something's been going on here,' he observed. He bent, noticing scraps of what appeared to be red fabric on the ground. 'I hate to say this, but wasn't Justine wearing a red tee-shirt?'

'Let me see that,' Jonathan said brusquely. He wrenched the tattered garment from Max's grasp, and held it close to his face, breathing deeply. 'It smells of her perfume. Max, what's happened to her?'

'I've no idea, though I could hazard a few guesses. Especially when you take this into consideration.' Max held up the remnants of Justine's bra. 'Looks like little Justine is running round the island topless, in the company of person or persons unknown.' He stood between the two poles and pushed at them with outstretched arms, testing their resilience experimentally. 'This whole place reeks of sex, don't you think?' he said absently.

'If you're suggesting that someone's had sex with Justine—' Jonathan began, worry etched across his face.

'That's exactly what I'm suggesting,' Max replied. 'And not the sort of sex you've been having with her, unless I'm very much mistaken. Still, it doesn't look like anything bad's happened to her.'

'You're right there,' Adrienne said. 'There are footprints leading out of this clearing, and there are obviously two sets of them. Whatever happened, it looks like when they left here he wasn't dragging her any more.'

'Well, in that case,' Max said, 'I reckon we keep following them.' He turned to his brother, who was still clutching the remains of Justine's tee-shirt. 'I just hope you're prepared for what we might find when we finally catch up with them.'

Chapter Six

Dusk was falling as Justine was led by her captor down a small slope towards his village. They could not have walked more than three miles from the spot in the forest where Justine had woken to find herself his prisoner, but the ground had been rough underfoot and their progress slow. She was hungry, filthy, bone tired and utterly fed up, still not quite able to believe what her senses were telling her – that somehow she had stepped back ten centuries in time, to an island which was still inhabited by the Vikings who had found a stopping place there.

The village itself was no more than a collection of little thatched huts, a storey high. A couple of goats were grazing on the scrubby grass, and distant smells of cooking floated on the twilight air. As Justine and the man trudged along the dusty path that led between the huts, heads began to emerge from doorways, gazing curiously at the newcomer. Justine tried to imagine how she appeared to them, her semi-clad body streaked with sweat and dirt from her exertions back at the dig and the punishment she had received in the woodland clearing. With her hands tied low in front of her, and her captor's tight hold on the rope, she could do nothing to shield her naked breasts from the villagers' curious gaze, and she felt a mixture of shame and excitement as lustful eyes bored into the pert little mounds.

In the centre of the village, they came to a halt. A small

circle of onlookers gathered around them, and Justine stared back defiantly as they approached. They were mostly men, dressed in the same fashion as the one who had kidnapped her, and sporting long hair and beards. A handful of women stood with them, wearing simple woven dresses, their hair braided, and gaudy beads hanging in strings around their necks and from the lobes of their ears. One of the women, bolder than the others, reached out a hand and stroked it over Justine's body, lingering for a moment on her breasts before moving down to tug at the waistband of her jeans, opening a couple of the buttons there in the process. It took a few seconds for Justine, expecting some kind of sexual overture, to realise that the woman was simply baffled: in this society females did not have short hair or wear trousers.

The man who had brought her into the village was deep in conversation with another, a heavy-set individual with deep crow's feet round his eyes and threads of grey in his red-gold hair. They spoke in a guttural language that was completely alien to Justine, but she knew that she was the subject under discussion from the way they gestured towards her every now and again. Even if she could have understood what was being said, her attention was distracted by the occasional curious hand, fondling her breast, or moving down over the denim-clad contours of her backside. One man reached for the fly of her jeans, attracted by the bright brass buttons. Justine braced herself for him to pull at them, but her captor had noticed, and the man's hand was sharply slapped away.

The older man seemed to have made some final decision, which did not appear to please her captor, as he shook his head and protested sharply. The two men stared at each other for a moment, her captor obviously hoping that the other would relent, but it seemed the conversation was at an end. Finally, reluctantly, he gave a yank on the rope that bound Justine's wrists, indicating that she was to follow him once more. She did as she was told, stumbling behind him towards a long, low hut, three times the size of any of the other little buildings. This, she knew from her studies of the Viking world, would be their great hall, where they would meet for feasts and formal occasions.

It seemed that almost everyone in the village had come with them, as Justine stepped inside, her nose wrinkling at the smell of old fires, roasted meat and stale sweat from drunken bodies. It was gloomy in here, and her eyes struggled to adjust to the dim light.

There was a raised dais at one end of the long hut, and Justine was led down to stand on it. The excited whispering which had marked her progress had not subsided; if anything, the interest in her seemed to be increasing. The villagers began to gather on the floor in front of her; she noticed that several of the men had girls in tow, who walked with their heads bent and their eyes downcast, every gesture suggesting the submissiveness of their nature. She suspected that if she could have seen their naked bodies, they would have been marked with the same bruises and weals her captor had so recently placed on her own backside, and she was alarmed to think that she might have inadvertently wandered into a world which handed out punishment on a routine basis. These girls were not the partners of the men they accompanied, Justine realised with a shudder of horror, but their possessions. There did not appear to be one woman in the room who was standing there independently of some man. This society was Max Cavendish's ultimate dream and her own nightmare: man the master, woman the slave.

She noticed three men conferring at the front of the little crowd; one of them, overweight and with the smooth, pink look of a pudgy, overgrown baby, was hefting a bag which jingled with the weight of the coins it held, and she knew exactly what he was intending to spend that money on. The outcome of the argument outside the hut became clear to her: the old man had told her captor that he had to sell her.

As she watched, the old man came to stand on the dais by her. He spoke a few brief words to her captor, and then went to sit on one of the benches that ran along the length of the wall.

The man came to stand beside her, and addressed the crowd. He sounded despairing, as though he would have done anything rather than make this speech, but there seemed to be no sympathy from the watching throng. The three men she had noticed watching her earlier seemed to take great delight in mocking him. One, in particular, had an answer for everything he said: the man was thin, with sharp features and dark, dead eyes. His hair was loose and lank, and his skin sallow. Don't let him be the one who buys me, Justine thought. I'll go with the overfed one with the pudgy face, or the clean-shaven blond if I have to, but not him.

Her captor unfastened the ropes that bound her wrists. She started to rub the soft skin there, flexing her fingers, but he caught hold of her hands and stilled her. He made a gesture, tugging impatiently at the waistband of her jeans, and Justine realised she was being ordered to take them off. She sat down on the hard wooden boards and removed her boots and socks, then slipped out of her jeans. She stood before the assembled crowd dressed in only her skimpy cotton panties, praying she would not be asked to remove those, too. As long as she still wore something, she felt she could retain a measure of dignity. Inevitably, she was ordered to remove those too.

He took hold of her hands and placed them on top of her head. She clasped her fingers obediently, aware that the movement raised and displayed her breasts more prominently. He ran his fingers over her nipples in a manner that was oddly possessive, and she felt the tender buds begin to stiffen under his touch. He smiled, pleased with the effect, and made some comment to the watching crowd. She almost expected him to open her mouth and prove to everyone that her teeth were healthy.

The three men who seemed to be paying her the most attention were muttering amongst themselves. The one she had taken an instant dislike to, with his thin moustache and lank hair, was gesturing towards the girl who sat patiently at his feet. He appeared to be offering her to one of his fellows, and Justine had the sudden, hideous presentiment that she would be replacing the passive, resigned-looking redhead in his household.

Her captor's hands had moved down, stroking roughly over her ribcage. There was a sharp comment, followed by a raucous laugh from the assembled purchasers, and Justine wished desperately she could understand what was being said about her; she wanted to answer back, though that was not possible, and would no doubt have earned her a beating for her pains if she had managed it.

Now he was pressing down on her stomach, and she felt a response in her uncomfortably full bladder, which she fought against as the fingers of his other hand snaked between her legs. At a word from the audience, he pushed at her thighs, wanting her to widen her stance. Mutely, she obeyed, feeling a digit parting her labia, seeking entrance to the depths of her sex. Still the pressure on her bladder continued; she wriggled, wanting to squeeze her thighs together and ease the discomfort. He stopped exploring between her legs long enough to slap her sharply on the bottom as a warning against movement.

Justine knew she was hideously close to wetting herself in front of everyone; she simply could not hold back any longer. She knew that if she tried to prevent it happening he would punish her, and she dreaded to think what the consequences would be if she did relieve herself. His probing finger was stimulating a spot somewhere on one of her inner walls that sent an urgent, burning sensation through her lower body, and she surrendered to the inevitable. A flush of mortification stained her cheeks as the liquid began to trickle out of her, the flow becoming a gush that soaked the Viking's hand and her own thighs. Around her, the crowd began to laugh, pointing and catcalling. Justine had never felt so ashamed.

'I'm sorry,' she mumbled, knowing he could not comprehend her. She watched as he put his sodden hand to his lips, and licked at it. His look was rueful as he spun her round, so that her back was to the audience, and bent her over. She suspected that this portion of his sales talk was planned – show the slave's breasts, belly, and sex, then offer her bottom as the finale – but she had not expected the heavy, stinging slap that descended on her unprotected backside. She yelped and struggled in his grasp, but she had already witnessed the Viking's strength this afternoon, and she knew it was futile to resist him.

More blows rained down, adding further pain to skin that was still tender from the earlier walloping it had received. His other hand twisted and tugged at her nipples, causing her to squeal. She was glad the watching crowd could not see the tears which sparkled in her eyes, although she was sure the sight of her most intimate areas, clearly visible to them between her parted legs, was of more immediate interest.

A voice called out. Justine was sure it belonged to the sharp-featured man who seemed most eager to acquire her services. At his words, her captor turned his attention to Justine's thighs, spanking the relatively well-covered back portion first, before aiming a couple of hard slaps at the tender inner flesh. Justine heard herself begging him to stop, her mind racing as she wondered whether anyone would come to save her from this ordeal. If Max were to appear in the doorway now, she told herself, she would fling herself at his feet and declare willing submission for as long as he desired, if only it would get her out of the clutches of these sadistic Vikings.

Abruptly, her punishment ceased, and she was once more turned to face her potential buyers. Her captor muttered a few words, and then the old man with the grey in his hair, who had been sitting a little apart from the others, rose to his feet. When he began to speak the room fell silent, and Justine knew his was the voice of true authority in this room. He gestured to Justine and her captor, and then turned to the three who had been discussing her merits among themselves. The demonstration of her charms was over: now it was time for them to put their money on the table.

The auction itself was swift, each man in turn seeming to offer an amount, which the next then considered briefly before raising. It was not long before the pudgy-faced one of the three dropped out, leaving the other two to haggle among themselves. At last the clean-shaven blond turned his palms upwards, indicating defeat; the face of his colleague broke into a sly grin, and Justine knew she had been sold to the one she dreaded. The two conferred amongst themselves, and then Sharp Features urged the redheaded girl to rise. When the girl went to sit at the blond's feet, Justine knew the extent of the bargain that had been struck to ensure Sharp Features succeeded in his bid.

Only one part of the ritual remained: Sharp Features reached into the folds of his breeches for his purse, counting out a number of silver coins into her captor's palm. Her captor counted them and nodded. Sharp Features caught Justine by the wrist and led her away, not even allowing her to pick up any of her fallen clothing. As she stumbled off the dais she looked back briefly to see her captor in a huddle with a couple of the other villagers, dividing up the money he had so recently earned and handing some of it to each. He glanced across and his eyes met Justine's. She could have sworn there was regret in his expression, and wondered whether it was because he had wanted to keep her for himself, or because he knew too well the nature of the man he had sold her to.

The little assembly in the hall was breaking up as Sharp Features led Justine away to her new life as a slave. His hut was on the far side of the village, a low wattle and daub building with a thatched roof, identical to all those which surrounded it. Justine's procession there did not attract the same attention as her arrival, even though she was now completely naked, her bare feet padding on the rough earth. It seemed that now her status had been decided, she had become as anonymous as any of the other slave girls here.

A girl of around Justine's own age was waiting in the doorway of Sharp Features' hut; at first Justine thought this might be his wife, until she saw the length of iron chain that circled the girl's ankle and tethered her close to the hearth. She had the same cowed, resigned expression as the redhead Sharp Features had traded in the hall, and the sight of Justine appeared to arouse no curiosity in her.

Sharp Features said something to the girl, who nodded, and led Justine inside. The hut's interior was not particularly spacious, and the timber and clay-like daub of the walls seemed to trap wood smoke from the fire and the lingering smells of cooking, under laid with a sour, more basic scent of unwashed male.

The girl motioned to Justine to sit on one of the wooden benches that lined the hut's walls. She was a pretty little thing, Justine thought, with strawberry-blonde hair caught in a knot at the back of her head, high cheekbones, widely-spaced blue eyes and a full-lipped mouth that gave her a sullen, sexy look, but her timid movements indicated that whatever spirit she had once possessed had been systematically crushed out of her.

There was an iron pot standing by the fire. The girl brought it over and Justine saw it was half-full of water. The girl fetched a piece of cloth, dipped it in the water, and began to wash Justine's limbs under the watchful eyes of Sharp Features. The water was surprisingly warm, even if the lye soap the girl was using smelt strongly of animal fat, and Justine closed her eyes and began to relax as the grime and dirt of her morning's work at the dig, together with the mixture of sexual secretions and urine, were cleansed from her skin. The girl seemed to be paying special attention to Justine's breasts, and she felt her nipples beginning to stiffen as the slightly rough cloth was rubbed over them. For the first time since she had been dragged away from her tent, she was being treated with sensuous affection, and she gave herself up to the girl's soft caresses. When the girl indicated that she should open her legs she did so without protest, and enjoyed the sensation of her vulva being gently washed.

There was the sound of something metallic clinking close to her, and Justine opened her eyes to see the girl holding a knife with a sharp-looking blade, and smiling. She tried to pull away, alarmed, but the girl shook her head and raised her own skirt towards her waist. Justine glanced up, to see a pair of legs that bore all the marks of a recent and prolonged beating, but it was the girl's sex that drew her attention. The plump little cushion of flesh was smoothly shaven, clearly revealing the neat slit that bisected it. So this was how Sharp Features, at least, liked his women. The girl dropped her skirt once more, lathered up the soap and began to spread it generously over Justine's mound of Venus. Taking the knife and bending close, she began to shear Justine's pubic hair away. This was a new sensation for Justine, and she sat stock still as the girl scraped the knife delicately over her skin. As the mixture of foam and hair was wiped away, Justine could see her own sex emerging beneath it, pink and new looking.

The girl was keeping Justine's sex lips apart with her fingers to make the task of shaving them easier. Justine had never been touched between her legs by another woman before, but the sensation was not unpleasant, and she was slightly disappointed when the girl pulled her fingers away for a moment.

She realised the girl was speaking to her, and shook her head. The girl patted her own chest and repeated the word.

'Gunvor.' She was introducing herself.

Justine mimicked the gesture. 'Justine,' she said, and Gunvor nodded and smiled.

She pointed in the direction of Sharp Features. 'Svein,' she said, before resuming her task.

Sharp Features – Svein, Justine amended mentally – was still watching, a lascivious smile on his face. He muttered something to Gunvor as the girl washed the last of the lather from Justine's now hairless quim. Gunvor glanced up at Justine, a mixture of fear and eagerness on her face, and bent to place a kiss between her fellow slave's legs; a kiss which deepened and intensified, the point of Gunvor's tongue running between Justine's labia to separate them.

Svein's expression was one of pure lechery, and Justine realised that this must be his other thrill, watching his slave girls pleasure each other. It seemed he was used to enjoying such a spectacle on a regular basis, for Gunvor, despite her relative youth, was highly skilled in the use of her tongue. Its warm, muscular tip circled Justine's clitoris, running over and over the sensitive little bud until Justine moaned and let her legs drape further apart. Despite the knowledge that Svein's eyes were fixed on her, Justine began to fondle her own nipples, titillating and toying with them until they stood rigid, the pink areolae crinkling around them.

Gunvor's tongue was dipping lower now, sliding down the moist furrow of Justine's sex and slipping briefly over her vaginal opening before working round to lap at her anus. Justine could not understand the fascination of this people for that musky rosebud, but Gunvor seemed more than happy to lick every inch of her fellow slave.

When Gunvor's tongue flickered over Justine's clit once

more, she could bear to be teased no longer. She caught hold of the girl's knot of hair and pulled her face closer to her quim. Not releasing her hold for a second, she whispered, 'I know you can't understand a word I'm saying, but please lick me till I come, Gunvor.'

The words were unnecessary; Gunvor had paid her oral tributes to Svein's redheaded slave for long enough to know when another girl was on the point of climax. Obediently, she carried on licking, gently pulling Justine's clit between her lips and sucking on it until Justine was frantic, her thighs clenching against the sides of Gunvor's head. At last Justine felt herself reach crisis point, and a burst of pleasure flared through her body, spreading out from her womb and causing her toes to curl and her skin to flush.

Finally, she released her grip on Gunvor's hair. The slave girl looked up at her anxiously, Justine's juices still glistening on her chin and lips. Have I pleased you? she was asking with her eyes.

'Thank you,' Justine whispered. She glanced across to Svein, gauging his reaction. His breeches, loose as they were, could not disguise the fact that he was erect. Justine prepared herself for him to drop his trousers and plunge that erection firmly into her channel, but it was not her body claiming his attention. Gunvor, her back still to her master, had raised her skirts once more, offering him a plain view of her dimpled buttocks and the dark, puckered hole between them.

He caught hold of Justine's arm and pulled her towards him. She did not know quite what she was expecting him to do, but she was still surprised when he heaved her over to a bed of straw in one corner of the hut and made her sit. He tossed her a dress of oatmeal-coloured wool, and waited while she put it on. Then he produced a length of chain, ending in a cuff similar to that which kept Gunvor tethered, and slipped it around Justine's ankle. Satisfied it was secure, he went back to Gunvor and tugged at her dress, which she began to remove. Justine curled herself into a ball on the straw and closed her eyes. Even with the grunts and groans Svein produced as he began to thrust his cock into Gunvor's body, it was not long before she was asleep.

Justine was woken by a none-too-gentle kick in the ribs. It took her a few moments to remember where she was, and then everything came flooding back: her capture in the forest, the slave auction, and her exploits with Gunvor. She opened her eyes and looked up to see Svein staring down at her, a lascivious expression on his sharp-featured face.

'Justine,' he said, having obviously learned her name from Gunvor. He added a few words she could not understand, and when she did not rise from where she was lying, he caught hold of her arm and jerked her into a sitting position. She glowered at him, picking pieces of straw from her short, blonde hair.

Beside her, Gunvor was sleeping. The girl's dress had nicked up around her bottom, and Justine noticed fresh-looking bruises on her fleshy white thighs.

Svein gestured to Justine, and mimed taking off clothes. Justine sighed and pulled her dress over her head. He smiled, and reached out to stroke her shoulders. His fingers were bony, and his touch slightly rough, but Justine did not pull away, much as she wanted to. He came to sit behind her, cupping her small breasts in his hands and pinching her nipples. Last night, when he had bought her, he had not laid a finger on her, leaving those duties to Gunvor, but now his hands were all over her, moving down the slight curve of her belly and delving between her legs. She thought back to the man who had taken her prisoner from the campsite; he had taken similar liberties, but she had accepted them because she sensed he enjoyed giving pleasure. Svein, on the other hand, was handling her as he might any of his possessions: if he fucked her, and she had no doubt that that was ultimately on his mind, he would only be interested in his own pleasure.

He urged her onto all fours, the position Gunvor had so readily adopted for him, and she did as he wished. Justine glanced back over her shoulder at him, trying to gauge his reaction to the sight of her arse cheeks and the groove of her sex, so blatantly displayed to him, but he was not standing behind her as she had expected. Instead, he was looking for something in a small wooden chest on the other side of the hut. Svein muttered something in satisfaction, and returned to her. She was alarmed to see he was holding what appeared to be a strap, fashioned from thick, dark hide, about a foot long. As he brought it close, flexing it in front of her face, she could see it was inscribed with Runic writing. If only Jonathan was here, she thought; he would know what it said. It was the first time she had thought about her boyfriend since she had found herself in this weird village; until now, she realised guiltily, she had only wondered how his brother would react when confronted with a society where the males were utterly dominant. She had to forget the strange hold Max Cavendish had acquired over her emotions: her future, if she had one, was pledged to Jonathan.

A sudden, dull pain spreading across her backside shocked her out of her train of thought. She had not felt the initial contact Svein's blow had made, but the aftershock made her want to leap to her feet. This time she heard the soft whistle of the strap, and tried to prepare herself mentally for its impact, but again she found a soft cry escaping her lips as the pain hit home. Max had told her that the strap was one of the milder implements he could have used on her; how would it feel if Svein was striking her with a whip, or a switch?

Blows were falling rhythmically on her unprotected rump. Svein was placing them so they landed one on top of the other, each wave of agony ebbing slightly only to flare up once more as the strap hit her tender flesh. Just when she thought she was beginning to accustom herself to the pattern of his assault, he sent a low blow along the underhang of her buttocks, and this time she did reach round and try to rub some of the soreness out of her skin. Angrily, Svein slapped her hands away.

Why are you doing this to me? she wanted to ask him. I've done nothing wrong. I haven't had a chance to do anything wrong. You're a sadist, Svein; you're not like Max. You don't care whether or not I enjoy what you're doing to me, and if you found out I didn't like it, you wouldn't stop.

His wrist flicked, and this time the flat of the strap curled between her buttocks and struck her sensitive sex lips. She yelped and rose to her feet, ignoring Svein's attempts to push her back into position. He shoved her to the ground and waved the strap under her nose. The supple hide shone with a familiar wetness. Justine found it hard to believe that her body could become so detached from her mind that it was receiving pleasure from her punishment, but here was the evidence.

Svein grunted and loosened the belt that held his trousers

in place. They dropped to his ankles, and for the first time Justine saw his long, thin cock. It was already partially erect, and a few strokes of his fist along its reddish length soon brought it to full hardness. He grasped Justine's hair and pushed her face down to the straw. He was just pressing the tip of his erection between her bruised and puffy labia when there was a commotion at the door. He muttered something, annoyed, and pulled his trousers back up. He aimed a kick at the prone Gunvor, and she sat up, rubbing her eyes sleepily.

Still with one hand in Justine's hair, Svein made his way to the door and yanked it open. The old man who had officiated at the auction was standing there, along with the pudgy-faced man who had been bidding for Justine. If they were aware of her nakedness, they did not comment. There was an angry exchange of words, and Pudgy Face pointed towards the horizon. Justine followed his gaze, and felt her heart lurch. Wandering down the rocky path towards the village were Max, Jonathan and Adrienne.

Chapter Seven

It had taken them longer than they thought to reach the end of the trail that should lead them to Justine. Night had fallen suddenly on Odinland, and none of them had thought to bring a torch. Only Max, used to living in the country, had had experience of anything like the utter darkness that descended on them. The moon was hidden behind low clouds and, afraid to go on over unfamiliar ground, and unable to retrace their steps without light to guide them, Max, Jonathan and Adrienne had simply huddled together in the bracken and slept fitfully, cold and hungry, and kept awake for long periods by the hooting of owls and the barking of foxes.

When dawn had come they had roused themselves, still weary and short-tempered. Max had been all for going back to the camp and having some breakfast, but Jonathan, increasingly afraid for Justine's safety, had insisted they press on. He was still worried by the remarks Max had made back in the forest clearing when they had found the scraps of clothing, and the way his brother had seemed to speak with authority on Justine and her sexuality. How on earth did Max know how she wanted to be treated? Surely she had not succumbed, somehow, to Max's charms? Jonathan had sworn, after what had happened with Vicky, that he was not going to let Max get his clutches on another of his girlfriends. But then he had said that after Diane, and Louise, and Rachel... If only he could understand what they all seemed to see in Max, who delighted in treating women as second-class citizens and was decadent enough to have ordered Anita to strip and be punished as the finale to the dinner party at his home.

Jonathan's mood of gloomy introspection had been broken when Adrienne, walking slightly in front of the two brothers, had called out that there was a village ahead.

'Are you sure?' he asked, breaking into a run to catch up with her.

'Take a look for yourself.'

The three of them stood at the crest of the hill, looking down on the cluster of little huts below them. There was no sign of any activity, but tethered goats and a patchwork of neatly tilled fields surrounding the village suggested it was not deserted.

'This is incredible,' Jonathan muttered, shielding his gaze from the early-morning sun with his hand. 'But I don't understand...'

'Neither do I,' Adrienne replied. 'You know and I know there isn't supposed to be anyone here. You don't think this is some kind of recent colony, do you? I mean, the Danes are pretty hot on recreating old Norse settlements.'

Jonathan shook his head. 'When I started planning this expedition I spoke to a Professor Mulstrup at the University of Copenhagen, and Fleming Sigmarsson, at the Centre for Cultural Studies in Oslo. Both of them told me their countries have made no attempt to find the remains of the Odinland settlement. They didn't exactly say so, but I think they still believe the island is cursed, and that's why they wouldn't come here.'

'I'm starting to think something pretty similar myself,' Max said dryly.

'So who in the hell is living here?' Adrienne asked.

'There's only one way to find out,' Jonathan said, and began to stride confidently down the hill in the direction of the village.

Adrienne grabbed hold of his arm. 'Jonathan, are you crazy? Anything could be waiting for us down there.'

'I know, but it's where Justine is, and I'm not turning back now.'

Adrienne gave a sigh, and began to follow Jonathan.

Max walked behind them at a slower pace, looking for any sign of the two men and the girl he had seen in the valley the day before. As they approached the village a young girl with pale ginger hair emerged from one of the huts. She caught sight of the little procession, screamed, and went running back inside. Men began to appear in doorways, talking amongst themselves. A couple of them went to bang on the door of another of the little dwellings. When its occupant answered, Jonathan was surprised to see he had a naked girl with him. A very familiar looking naked girl.

'Justine!' he called, and sprinted the last hundred yards into the village. He found himself confronted by a group of seven or eight men, their expressions a mixture of aggression and fear. None of them, however, appeared to be carrying a weapon.

One of the villagers, a man in his fifties, with long red-gold hair that was fading to grey, addressed him. It took Jonathan a moment to realise he was speaking a very old, very pure form of Norse dialect.

'Who are you?' the man repeated.

'My name is Jonathan,' he replied haltingly, his brain attempting to form words he had seen written down many times, but had only heard in taped readings of the sagas he had taught his pupils. Even as he spoke, his mind was struggling to cope with the implications. If these were modern-day colonists, as Adrienne had suggested, they would have been speaking Norwegian or Danish, or even English, not some language that had died out nearly a thousand years earlier. 'I believe you have a friend of mine,' he added.

'Where have you come from?' the man asked.

'We have a camp on the other side of the island,' Jonathan told him. 'Ask the person who came to it, and stole our friend away.'

The old man turned to another, a younger man with the same oval face, high cheekbones and golden-red hair. 'Is this true, Erik? Is that where you found the girl?'

The younger man nodded. 'She was a stranger, and she was alone. I did not see any of these others with her. It seemed a good opportunity, and you know why I needed her...'

'Jonathan!' He turned at the sound of Justine's voice. She was standing at the side of a thin, sharp-faced man with lank, dark red hair. She was no longer naked, but wore a woollen dress that seemed too large for her small frame. Her feet were bare, and what shocked Jonathan the most was that there was a metal cuff around her ankle, to which a length of chain was obviously meant to be attached.

'Justine? Are you all right?' he asked, walking towards her.

'I suppose so, if you can call being tied up, beaten, fucked up the arse and then auctioned off to a sadistic Viking bastard all right.'

Jonathan was appalled. 'Tied up? Beaten? What are you talking about?'

103

Max and Adrienne came to join the little group. 'What's going on?' Max asked.

'That's what I'm trying to find out,' Jonathan replied. He noticed that the villagers no longer seemed to be paying him any attention. Instead, they seemed captivated by Adrienne. The old man who had been talking to Jonathan reached out and touched her, drawing his fingers along the length of her arm wonderingly. The smooth black sheen of her skin seemed to be what was fascinating him.

'Your woman,' he said eventually. 'I had heard stories of the Nubians, but I never thought to see one.'

'Do you mind?' Adrienne asked, breaking into the conversation with a slightly less faltering grasp of Norse than Jonathan had shown. 'I am no Nubian, and I am certainly not his woman.'

'You have spirit,' the old man laughed. He turned to Max. 'She must be yours, then. Is she for sale?'

'What's he saying?' Max asked Jonathan.

'He wants to buy Adrienne off you,' Jonathan replied.

'Buy her?' Max was bemused.

'That seems to be how things work around here,' Jonathan told him. 'It looks like the bloke with the moustache has already bought Justine.'

'You're joking, aren't you?' Max said. 'Either that, or I'm still asleep.'

'Just let me sort this out, Max.' Jonathan knew that, for once, he was in charge and Max would have to follow his lead. It was a strange, not unpleasant feeling. He turned back to the leader of the villagers. 'Old man…' he began.

'Call me Einar,' the man replied.

'Einar, we have a lot to talk about. The release of my friend, for one thing.'

'Ah…' Einar looked grave. 'I think we should discuss

this over some food. I for one have not yet broken fast today. Come with me, all of you.'

Jonathan and Adrienne began to follow him, gesturing to Max, who was unable to follow the conversation, to come with them. Jonathan hoped Justine would join them, too, but the sharp-faced man dragged her away. He cast a long, despairing look at her as she was bundled back into one of the huts.

It was cramped inside Einar's home, but Max and Jonathan found room on a hard wooden bench. When Adrienne went to sit with them the old man cast Jonathan a querying look. There was already a fair-haired girl, dressed in the same kind of woollen outfit Justine had been wearing, sitting patiently on the floor, and Jonathan realised Einar was expecting Adrienne to take her place at the men's feet.

'Like she said, she isn't my woman, and she doesn't sit on the floor,' Jonathan told him. He watched as Einar told the girl to go and prepare food for his guests. She rose to her feet without complaint and began to busy herself by the hearth. 'Now, tell us what all this is about,' he said.

Einar gestured to his younger companion. 'My son, Erik, found the girl on the other side of the island, as he said. She did not appear to belong to anyone, and so he claimed her as his prize.'

'So what's she doing with the man with the moustache?' Jonathan asked, aware that Adrienne was translating the gist of the conversation for Max's benefit.

'That is Svein, the silversmith,' Einar said. 'He bought the girl from Erik.'

'Not because I wanted to sell her,' Erik said angrily. 'She should be mine still.'

'You had no choice,' Einar told his son. 'You see, Erik

105

likes to gamble, but he ran up debts he could not afford to pay. Svein was more than generous in the money he offered for the girl, and now Erik's debts are paid off.'

So that explained what Justine had said about the auction, but there were still questions Jonathan needed answering. He paused for a moment as the slave girl handed round plates containing flat rye bread, soft cheese and fruit, and iron cups containing a sharp, honeyed drink, then turned to Erik. He studied the man for a moment, taking in his strong, muscular build and powerful physical presence. It was easy to see how he could have overpowered the small, slender Justine without effort. 'Justine said you beat her, and – and fucked her. Why did you do that?'

'Because it turns him on, presumably,' Max muttered. 'Why else would anyone do it?'

'I told you,' Erik said. 'She was mine. I had claimed her. And she was not unwilling, whatever she might have told you.'

'Well, whoever she might or might not belong to, I want her back,' Jonathan said.

'That might not be your decision to make,' Einar said, spitting a cherry stone in the direction of the hearth. 'She is the property of Svein now, and he may not want to sell her.'

Jonathan rose to his feet, his food largely untouched. 'Well let's go and find out, shall we?'

'You're a fool if you think I'll give you the girl,' Svein said with a sneer. He stood in the doorway of his hut blocking Jonathan's access, but the young archaeologist could vaguely see Justine in the dim interior, kneeling anxiously by the fire. 'I paid good money for her, and

I'm not about to give her up without recompense. If you can match what I paid for her, I'll think about it.'

'How can I do that?' Jonathan asked. 'I don't have any money — at least, nothing that would be of any use to you.'

'I'd take silver, or precious stones,' Svein suggested.

'We don't have any of those, either,' Jonathan said.

'Well, if you have nothing with which to bargain, we have nothing further to discuss. Justine is mine, and I shall continue to do with her as I wish.' He made to turn his back on Jonathan, then changed his mind. 'The girl doesn't understand a word I say. Tell her to come here.'

Jonathan found himself harbouring a deep dislike for the weasel-like Svein, with his disdainful arrogance, but he did as the man asked, knowing it might give him an opportunity to talk to Justine. He pushed past the jeweller and beckoned to Justine.

'Svein wants to see you,' he said.

'What does he want?' Justine asked, brushing her hair out of her eyes.

'I don't know,' Jonathan replied.

'Tell her to bring the cuffs,' Svein called from the doorway. 'They are in the box on the topmost shelf.'

Jonathan relayed his orders to Justine, who paled visibly but did as she was told. As she approached Svein, he wrenched the iron cuffs from her grasp and quickly secured them around her wrists.

'And now she comes with me,' Svein said. 'Follow if you wish, but there is nothing you can do. If you try to take her from me, I can have you killed. It is the law of this island that if a man wishes to take his slave to the punishment post, and has good reason to do so, no other man can lay a hand on him until the punishment is completed.'

'But you don't have any reason to punish Justine,' Jonathan retorted, fighting the rising desire to clamp his hands around Svein's throat and squeeze the sneering smile off his face.

'Of course I do. She does not obey my orders. I tell her to do something, and she simply looks at me.'

'That's because she can't understand what you're asking her to do,' Jonathan snapped with a mixture of exasperation and frustrated fury. 'You've already told me as much yourself. You're just looking for an excuse to do whatever you want with her.'

'Her behaviour does not satisfy me, and that is not good enough. A session at the punishment post will teach her that obedience is all.' Svein attached a short length of chain to the cuffs around Justine's wrists. 'Stand aside, stranger,' he ordered. He pushed roughly past Jonathan and the others and began to walk away, dragging Justine with him. Her bare feet stumbled on the stony earth, and Jonathan felt his heart lurch. He couldn't let this arrogant Norseman hurt her; he had to do something, however futile the gesture might prove.

'What's happening now?' Max asked. 'Where's he taking Justine?'

'To a punishment post, wherever that might be,' Jonathan replied.

'I know exactly where it is,' Max said. 'It's where I saw the people I was telling you about yesterday. We'd better go after him.'

'Why?' Jonathan asked, turning angrily on his brother. 'Because you think you can help Justine, or because you want to watch? You'll enjoy it, won't you, Max, seeing whatever punishment he decides to hand out. That's how you get your kicks, isn't it?'

'Jonathan, calm down.' Max placed a hand on Jonathan's arm. 'I know you're upset about this, and scared, but taking it out on me isn't going to help. You may not like it, but at least I know how that Svein character's mind works, and I don't agree with what he's going to do, if that's any consolation to you. I want to stop him just as much as you do, but if we start fighting among ourselves we're not going to get anywhere. Now come on, let's get out of here.'

Jonathan and Max ran out of the village, following Svein. Jonathan had considered asking Adrienne not to come with them, not wanting her to get caught up in a possible fight, but she seemed determined, as did Erik, the man who appeared to have caused the whole mess in the first place. Still, he thought as he jogged along the dusty path trying to ignore a growing stitch in his side, there's safety in numbers, and we may need all the help we can get.

By the time Jonathan came to a halt before the punishment post, Svein was already making his preparations. Erik had led them on the shortest route to the valley, but Jonathan's bickering with Max had given the silversmith a good head start.

Svein was in the process of removing Justine's wrist cuffs. He looked round, smiling. 'Nice try, stranger, but you're too late. I'm in the circle now, and you can't do anything till I come out of it.'

Jonathan looked across, and realised there was a circle of flat white stones, each about the size of a saucer at a distance of three metres or so from the central post. They marked out an area where the yellowish earth had been firmly tramped down.

'What is this place?' Jonathan asked Erik. 'Why is it so special?'

'In the village punishments take place all the time, but they are minor and no one remarks upon them,' Erik replied. 'It is just a part of our everyday life. Occasionally, a man might need to give his woman a punishment which is more severe, to teach her a lesson he does not want her to forget, or because she has made some transgression which carries a greater penalty than a slap of the hand or a couple of stripes with his belt. Or he may wish to sell her to another man, and that man will ask for a demonstration of what he will be getting for his money. There are many reasons why a slave might deserve a public beating, and this is where such beatings take place. As Svein said, once a man steps within the circle of stones, then no one can prevent him from carrying out such punishment as he feels his slave deserves. I am afraid that until he crosses the line once more you cannot stop him from doing what he wants, and if you try to go into the circle he can order you to be put to death.'

Jonathan relayed the information to Max, who replied grimly, 'Well the second he comes out of that bloody circle it's four against one, and I don't fancy his chances.'

'Yes, but until then we've got to stand back and just watch him,' Jonathan complained. 'We're not Vikings, for God's sake; we don't have to obey their stupid rules.'

'We might have to, if we want to get off this island in one piece,' Adrienne said. 'Come on, Jon, you know all about the Viking code of honour. These people are men of their word, and if they say you'll be killed if you cross the circle, they mean it. Svein might be a nasty piece of work, but he's got more friends in the village than we have, and if he hasn't got friends, then I bet he's got people who owe him favours, or money, like Erik here. If he wanted someone to do away with us, I reckon they'd have no qualms about doing it. I don't know about you, but I really don't want to risk that happening.'

'Are you watching, stranger?' Svein asked, mockingly. 'Are you ready for the punishment to begin?' As he spoke he tugged the dress down off Justine's shoulders and arms, letting it fall in a little heap around her feet. Jonathan stifled a gasp as he looked at Justine's naked body. He was not prepared for the sight of her shaven sex; her eyes followed his gaze, and she tried to shield herself with her hands until Svein pulled them away. Jonathan felt a slight stiffening in his groin, and realised that something in Justine's vulnerability was turning him on. It didn't make any sense, he told himself. He had always treated Justine as an equal, as he had done with all his other girlfriends. He had never found any enjoyment in treating women as his inferiors, and he had never felt a desire to assert any kind of dominance over them. So why was he suddenly becoming excited at the moment when she was at her most helpless?

Svein was busily fastening Justine's hands into the thick iron cuffs that dangled at the end of the chains attached to the posts. She was not a particularly tall girl, and certainly she must have been shorter than the average female on this island, for when the cuffs were secured in place her arms were stretched full length above her head, and her toes made the barest contact with the ground beneath them. She appeared to be struggling to hold herself in that position, and Max whispered in Jonathan's ear, 'This doesn't look good, you know.'

'What makes you say that?' Jonathan asked, alarmed by Max's tone of voice.

111

'Well, she's not going to be able to stay like that if he starts hitting her. The chains will carry her weight, but...' He broke off as Svein stood back to admire his handiwork.

'She's a beautiful girl, this Justine,' Svein observed, running his hands casually over her body. 'Her skin will mark well, I think.'

'I'm going to kill him,' Jonathan muttered, his hands clenching into involuntary fists.

'Look, Jon, he's not going to do anything too severe to her,' Max reassured him. 'The men here rely on the women to do the menial work for them. They'd never do anything that would prevent a slave from carrying out her duties.'

'I don't care,' Jonathan retorted. 'It's the pleasure he's taking in taunting us like this that's really annoying me.'

'Beautiful, beautiful skin,' Svein crooned, as if the words were some obscene lullaby. 'Perfect for bearing the outline of a palm.' As he spoke he brought the flat of his hand down on Justine's left buttock, the sound of the smack reverberating in the quiet valley. She flinched, but stifled any greater reaction. Jonathan thought of the scene at Max's, when he had chastised Anita in a similar fashion. Then, his brother had prepared his girlfriend for what was to come. Svein had obviously considered such niceties to be unnecessary.

'Come closer,' Svein suggested. 'Surely you cannot see what I'm doing from that distance. You cannot take in every little detail of how Justine's flesh has reddened. Come close, so you will be able to feel the heat as it rises from her skin.'

He punctuated his words with more slaps, alternating between Justine's bottom cheeks. Despite Svein's assumptions, Jonathan could indeed begin to see the mottled discolouration on Justine's skin. He did not need to stand any closer to realise he was looking at the outlines of the silversmith's long, bony fingers.

Max had been right about one thing; the force of the spanking was causing Justine to wobble precariously on her tiptoes as she sought purchase on the sandy ground. This was not to Svein's liking, and he clasped her tightly around the waist with his right hand as he continued to belabour her buttocks with his left. After a few moments of this a thought appeared to cross his mind, and he altered his stance. This time when he held her, his right hand was between her legs. It was an awkward-looking position, and he was unable to hit her quite as hard as he had been doing, but Jonathan knew that was not the point. Svein wanted them all to see that his hand was in Justine's most intimate place. From the way he was holding her, Jonathan suspected he had at least one finger inside her quim, and the idea caused a mixture of anger and humiliation to churn in his guts.

His suspicions were confirmed when Svein withdrew his hand and made a great show of licking his middle finger. 'Like all true slaves, her juices flow when she is being punished,' he said. 'Although she knows she has done wrong, she still takes pleasure in her pain. She cannot help it.'

'You've proved your point, now let her go,' Jonathan replied. He was surprised to discover his erection was still pulsing and lengthening, despite his anger, and he remembered how he had felt the same sensations when he had watched Anita being spanked by Max. On that occasion, though, he had been able to take Justine up to the guest bedroom and sink his cock deep into her pussy. Here, there was nothing he could do except try to deny his growing, unfathomable excitement.

'Let her go? I have not even started yet,' Svein answered. He let go of Justine, who had already given up the fight to keep her feet on the ground. She hung in her bonds, letting the heavy iron chains bear the weight of her body.

As Jonathan watched, Svein took something from his belt and uncoiled it. He realised it was a thin whip, the best part of eighteen inches long. Justine had seen it, too. Her eyes widened, but she said nothing. There was nothing she could say, Jonathan thought; at least, nothing Svein could understand.

Svein stood for a moment, surveying the tempting target with which Justine's bottom presented him. He smiled, half to himself, making a great show of twisting the whip between his hands. Just get on with it, Jonathan wanted to shout. Don't torture her like this. Don't torture me.

Suddenly the whip arced through the air, landing with a discernible crack on Justine's backside. She cried out, and Jonathan realised he had been holding his breath. A thin red line sprung up on Justine's flesh, but what worried him more was the fact that, as she instinctively moved away from the man who was punishing her, her body had begun to twist in its chains, the metal links coiling around each other and lifting her further off the ground as they tightened. When Svein brought the whip down again, as he was clearly intending to do, there was no guarantee it would land on her buttocks.

However, the silversmith seemed to be more skilled with the whip than Jonathan had suspected, timing the second blow so that it landed as Justine swung towards him, and left a second line on her buttocks, parallel to the first. Again she yelped, her body slowly rotating in mid-air.

Perhaps Svein was more careless this time, or perhaps he simply wanted to raise the stakes. He struck out as

Justine twisted away from him and the whip snaked round and caught her on the top of her thigh. This time her cry was more full-blooded. Jonathan, watching impotently, could only clench his fists in frustration. He wanted desperately to snatch the whip from Svein's hand and bring it down on the man's back, letting him know how it felt to have his skin abused by the thin, supple leather thong. And then, he realised with guilty shock, he would take the opportunity to discover for himself how it felt to use the implement on his girlfriend...

'If I could only get my hands on that whip,' he muttered.

'Same here,' Max replied, an odd, faraway expression on his face. 'I wondered how long it would take you to come round to my way of thinking.'

Justine cried out again. Svein was swinging the whip with relentless regularity now, the weals criss-crossing on her bottom cheeks and curving round her thighs. Jonathan could see that, on a couple of occasions, the tip of the whip had curled into the soft, sensitive flesh only inches from her sex.

Justine's body was swinging a little more wildly now, propelled by the force of the blows that Svein was raining down on it. Her eyes were half-closed, and tendrils of her short blonde hair were sticking to her face. She seemed utterly resigned to accepting the punishment Svein was inflicting on her.

The only sounds in the quiet valley were the whistling as the whip cut through the air, followed by Justine's moans and gasps as it landed; strange noises somewhere between supplication and ecstasy. The silversmith had laid stripes across her stomach, too, and Jonathan knew with some secret instinct that his next target would be her small, high breasts. The thought of seeing the whip land on that tender flesh sent a shudder of perverse pleasure through him, and he tried to fight the feeling. He should be protecting Justine from this punishment, not colluding in it.

'I think that's enough,' Svein muttered, and let the whip fall from his hand. Justine hung limply in her bonds, her chest rising and falling as she sobbed quietly. Svein ran a hand over the raised red marks on her backside, laughing as she tried to move away from his touch. 'Or maybe not…'

Swiftly, he removed her from the wrist cuffs, helping her down to the ground. If Jonathan thought the man would simply hand her back her dress and let her return to the village, he was wrong. Svein's next action was to drop his woollen trousers to his knees, revealing his partially erect penis. He put a hand on Justine's head, pressing her down to her knees, and stood before her, waiting.

Justine glanced over at Jonathan for the briefest of moments, and then caught hold of Svein's shaft, bending her head to take the tip of his glans between her lips. Once his cock was in place Svein caught hold of her hair, holding her steady, and then began to drive in and out of her mouth, as deep as he could go. When he judged that this technique had brought him to the desired hardness he pulled out and pushed her to the ground. He spread her legs, and Jonathan could clearly see the pink wetness of her sex, open and ready, as Svein prepared to straddle her.

'How can she bear to let him touch her?' Adrienne asked Max.

'She's probably imagining he's Jon or me,' Max replied.

In any other circumstances Jonathan would have considered those to be fighting words, but he needed his brother as an ally if he was to rescue Justine from this predicament. For now, all he could do was watch helplessly as Svein positioned the head of his cock at the entrance to Justine's vagina, and slowly plunged it into her tight, hot depths. Obviously feeling the need to demonstrate his continued mastery of her, he caught hold of her hands and held them over her head as he began to thrust. The ground must have been rough against Justine's abused back and buttocks, Jonathan thought, but she seemed not to notice. Her eyes were half-closed as she moved beneath Svein, following his rhythm with jerking motions of her hips. It was not long before the silversmith's buttocks gave one last heave, and he spent his seed inside Justine's body. She gave a small, guttural cry that Jonathan recognised as the indication that she, too, had reached orgasm, and then lay, too weak to protest, as Svein withdrew and wiped his cock on her discarded dress.

At last, Svein stepped out of the circle of stones which surrounded the punishment post. He came so close to Jonathan that the young archaeologist could smell his sour breath as he spoke. 'You see how she responds to me?' he said. 'She cries out in pleasure, and welcomes me into her body. You have lost her, stranger. She no longer wants you.'

Jonathan had had enough of the man's taunts. He flung himself at Svein, fists flying, and was gratified to feel a couple of his blows land. Before he could inflict any serious damage on the silversmith he was pulled away by Erik and Max.

Svein hauled Justine to her feet, blood dripping from a cut above his eye, and began to drag her away. 'That was a foolish thing you did, stranger,' he called back over his shoulder. 'A very foolish thing.'

'I had to do it,' Jonathan panted, wriggling free of Erik's strong grasp. 'The bastard deserved it. There was no need for what he did to Justine.'

Erik shook his head. 'You have much to learn about the way we behave here, Jonathan. Perhaps it will make things easier for you to understand if I tell you a little about the history of this island.'

Chapter Eight

'My father's father's fathers came to this island more years ago than anyone can count,' Erik began, settling himself on one of the low wooden benches in Einar's hut. 'They were searching for the Green Land that Erik the Red had found and claimed for our people, but they were forced to rest on this shore when a violent storm threatened their ship, and they found a home here.

'The leader of the expedition was a lazy but very handsome man, Magnus Yellowhair. He was not popular with some, for he was a daydreamer, always with some idle thought in his head, and the lust for blood was not in him. His true failing, however, was that he was too fond of the women; he was always to be found between the legs of one or other of the village maidens, and it was said that he was sent away on the voyage because he had seduced the daughter of one of the elders, who was being groomed for marriage to a neighbouring warlord, and got her with child. And who would want a woman who was carrying another man's child?

Of course, Magnus was soon up to his old tricks once the longboat set sail. By the time they had journeyed halfway to their destination, he had lain with almost every woman on the ship who was of age. And none of them objected, though there were a few of the men who would have happily cut his throat while he slept. If one of them had done, who knows how different things would have been for us?

There was one maiden on the ship whose name was Mette, and she had just turned sixteen years old. She had a young, fresh beauty, with hair the colour of ripe corn and eyes bluer than the water in the deepest fjords, and Magnus was determined that she should be his, not just for the duration of the voyage, but for life. She was under the guard of her father, who was all too aware of Magnus' reputation. But the man fell sick for several days, and in that time Magnus made his move.

Of course, Mette herself knew all about Magnus, for the tales of his sexual prowess had spread rapidly among the women on board, but she was intrigued by his good looks and his beguiling charm, and eagerly she consented to be alone with him once night fell.

The girl was a virgin, but she was not afraid when Magnus began to kiss her, and then to strip her of her clothes. She was curious, and wanted nothing more than to feel his hard, young body lying on top of hers, possessing her completely. And so he did, night after night. He taught Mette all the pleasures of sex, and she learned quickly.

No one knows when he first thought to use his hands on her plump little arse. It was not uncommon among our people for a man to chastise his woman if she had done something wrong, for there was nothing worse than a woman who rose above her place. But Magnus realised that if he laid his palm across Mette's backside it gave her great pleasure, and she would respond to his caresses with more enthusiasm than usual.

It was only once the ship was landed that Magnus and Mette's relationship began to change into something that had never been seen before. Her father, naturally, was not happy with what was happening; if he could have chosen any husband for his daughter it would most certainly have not been the indolent womaniser, Magnus Yellowhair. However, Mette insisted she loved Magnus, and she would not be parted from him.

It had become obvious by now that the settlers had no intention of travelling on to the Green Land. This little island, which they named after Odin, the father of our gods, was fruitful, and a good place to live. Magnus, also, was enjoying the power he had had on board ship, and he did not want to relinquish that power to the village elders in the Green Land settlements. And for all his faults, he made a fair leader, and the people were happy enough.

Mette and Magnus still played their bed games, but he soon began to realise she craved more than just the occasional spanking. Mette seemed to want to submit utterly to his will, and he realised that he took pleasure in making her bend to his desires. He had a power over her that derived from her own needs, and he revelled in that power. Other men, it seemed, hurt their women by punishing them, but Magnus knew that the way to hurt Mette was not to punish her.

I know you understand this situation, Jonathan, for it seems your brother is a man such as Magnus was, but at first the other men in the village could not understand why Mette was so obedient. They had women who nagged them, or who were idle about the house, or who had lost pleasure in lying with them, and yet here was Magnus Yellowhair, happy and contented, with his woman who did as he bid her, and who had not lost the joy of feeling his thick member penetrate her body.

When Magnus explained to them that Mette took pleasure in being punished, they could not understand what he meant. Their own women were frightened of the angry voice and the raised fist that came before a beating. And when Magnus told them that he beat Mette because he loved her, and because she had chosen to be his chattel, they were even more puzzled. So he arranged a demonstration of what he meant. He took Mette to the outskirts of the forest, along with those who were curious to see what he meant to do.

He stripped the dress from Mette's body, and the men gasped to see the beauty of her full breasts and plump bottom. Patiently she stood while he tied her wrists to the lowest branches of a young tree, so that her arms were outstretched above her head, and then he took the belt from around his waist and used it to beat her naked body.

The men who watched were at first outraged to see this, for in her bound and helpless position Mette could not defend herself in any way. But they became amazed by what they witnessed, for though she cried out as the belt fell again and again, raising red weals on her creamy skin, she did not try to escape from the source of the pain and her cries slowly began to change to those of a woman who is in the throes of great passion. Indeed, when Magnus dropped the belt to the ground, his arm weary, Mette pleaded with him to continue, her love for him and her need for punishment were so strong.

Of course, the men of the village became excited by what they had seen, and many of them rushed back to their homes, pulled their women away from whatever chore they were doing and took them then and there. Gradually they began to follow Magnus' example, and the women came to believe it was their role to be the slave, and their man's role to be the master.

The change, once it began, was very swift. The blood

lust and need to conquer the weak that had driven our people grew less. We turned from the gods we used to worship, like Tyr the warrior. There seemed no point in celebrating the joys of fighting and killing when we no longer embraced such a concept in our lives. Our prayers were offered to Lofn, the goddess of passion, and Thor, the god of thunder, whose protection we sought from the fierce storms that would threaten the island in winter.

We saved our moment of greatest worship for the midsummer solstice. On that night every man and woman on the island would come together in a celebration of our love for each other, and for the gods who guarded us. It would be a wild night, full of feasting and music and dancing, and it would culminate with a ritual in which all the men of the village would punish the womenfolk, and then they would lie with them. It was not necessarily husband who punished wife, either, for as you know, a man can feel a need to lie with more than one woman, and on midsummer night he would be given sanction to seek whichever partner he chose.

It was on one such midsummer's night that their lives were altered forever. Magnus and his clan had gone out into the woods, and lit fires. Their children were sleeping soundly under the stars, lulled to sleep by the soft music of our pipes and drums. They had eaten well, killing the fattest boar and roasting it till its skin was crisp and its meat was succulent. And then they had begun the ritual. One by one, every woman disrobed and stood before the fire, the flames reflecting on their naked skin. Each man would then choose the one who would be his for the night. Such a selection it was; some tall and slender as reeds, others small and delicate of limb. Some with corn-coloured hair, others with tresses the red of autumn leaves.

Some with large, hanging breasts and fat, dimpled backsides that cried out to be beaten, others with breasts you could cover with your hands and arses as tight and perfect as a boy's. No man could look at that array of beauty and not want to claim it for his own.

One by one, the couples peeled off. Some went deep into the woods to celebrate the night in greater privacy, but most stayed close to the fire. Magnus, a man in middle age now, began the proceedings. His partner would not have been Mette, of course, but perhaps one of the village maidens, for he had never lost his liking for pretty young girls. With her hands bound behind her back, she stood, patient as a statue, while he brought his hand down on her un-protesting backside. It was an honour to be chosen for this ritual beating by Magnus, and the maiden's status as a slave would be greatly enhanced if she could bear these blows without flinching.

Once the imprint of his palm was clearly visible on her fleshy cheeks, Magnus took the ceremonial whip that was used only on these occasions. It was longer and thinner than the whips with which slaves would usually be punished, and it took skill to lay stripes which would mark, but not scar. Magnus was the expert in these matters, and by the time he had finished, the girl would have vivid red weals crossing her back and arse, but he would not have broken the skin once.

Of course, it was much harder for her to bear the whipping in silence, and the silent woods would echo to her cries as the supple leather bit into her flesh. Despite the severity of the pain she felt, however, it would not be unknown for such a girl to fall to her knees at the end of her punishment and beg for more. We Vikings can endure any pain, for if we cannot do this, what right have we to inflict such treatment on others?

Those who watched this performance were not unmoved by it, and by the time Magnus threw his whip to the ground there were many men watching who had their fingers buried deep between the sex lips of their slaves, or who had their manhood held lovingly in a woman's fist.

The pitch of the music had risen, and many of the villagers were intoxicated, not only by the mead they had drunk, but by the fierce rhythm of the drumming. The men now fell on their women, chastising them with their hands, or their belts. Everywhere, there were moans and gasps, first of pain, but gradually turning to sweet, wild pleasure.

And suddenly there were strangers in the midst of the revels, a scouting party from the Green Land, who had finally become curious about this little island and had wondered if perhaps it held a clue to the whereabouts of that boatload of voyagers, led by Magnus Yellowhair, who had become lost somewhere en route to their own settlement.

Why they came so late in the night, I do not know. Perhaps they, like us, were hampered and delayed by the treacherous currents that surround this island. Perhaps their true intention was to rape and pillage, and they had wanted the element of surprise to aid them. Whatever, they could not have chosen a worse time to come upon us. All around, they were confronted with the evidence of men and women in thrall to their passions. Some women lay on their backs with their legs wide while their lover swived them; others were on their hands and knees, rutting as the animals do. Hands and mouths caressed breasts and cunnies, and everywhere the women bore the evidence of the beatings they had enjoyed, their skin reddened and marked with weals. Here and there, some even gave themselves up to the attentions of their lovers with their hands still bound.

It was too much for these raiders, who knew nothing like it in their own country. They could, of course, have chosen to slaughter everyone they found, for no Viking warrior was ever afraid to kill a defenceless victim. The legends say that indeed many of those children who they had found sleeping in the woods were slaughtered, and that they moved to strike at Magnus and his people with their knives and axes, but a sudden, violent storm blew up. The island was shaken by bolts of lightning that set fire to the tops of trees, and lit up the sky in crazy patterns of searing white light. Thunder rumbled high overhead, louder and more frightening than anyone had known it, and the rain came down like a thousand fists, punching the fight from the strangers.

The island people were not afraid, for they knew that their years of obeisance to Thor had earned them this protection. The thunder god had come to protect their people at the moment they were most in need of it.

The members of the scouting party turned and fled for the beach, afraid that their longboat would be torn apart by the ferocity of the storm. Magnus and the village men ran after them, still naked, and taunted them with their cowardice. It was a foolish thing to do.

The leader of the scouts turned and confronted Magnus. He told him that his people would be damned for turning away from the old ways, and that he would make sure no one ever knew of the evil ceremonies which took place on the island. The last thing they did before they sailed for home was to smash the longboat which had brought

Magnus and his party here. They wanted to make sure the islanders would not leave, though by then I doubt that anyone would have wanted to. And those were the last strangers to set foot on these shores until you arrived.'

There was a long silence after Erik's story came to its conclusion.

'Well, that certainly explains a few things,' Jonathan eventually said. 'Like why the Vikings tried to destroy everything that had ever been written about this place, and why they spread the stories that it was deserted and cursed. They really didn't want anyone to find you.'

'That may be the case, but there are many things that still have to be explained about you,' Erik said. 'Max and Justine, why don't they speak our language?'

Jonathan took a deep breath. 'Erik, I don't know how to tell you this, but this island is the only place in the world where anyone speaks your language. Adrienne and I only know what we know because we've studied it.'

'But you told me you are from England. My people are strong in England...'

'Not any more,' Jonathan replied. 'I'm sorry, Erik, but the Vikings didn't conquer the world. They tried, but their enemies became more powerful, and their religion was wiped out by kings who were part of the Christian faith. The gods you worship are just about forgotten, except in legends and stories. Everything's different now.'

Erik buried his head in his hands, trying to come to terms with what he was hearing. 'This cannot be,' he said finally. 'How could it happen?'

'Perhaps it's Thor's final revenge,' Jonathan said. 'By cursing Magnus and the islanders to extinction, all the raiders did was curse themselves. Your people survived, but theirs were overthrown. It all makes a strange, ironic kind of sense, if you think about it.'

'So what happens now?' Erik asked.

'Well, we go back to America, and we tell no one that you're still alive,' Jonathan said. 'You can just carry on living your lives in peace, as if we'd never set foot here. Actually, I'd hate to think what would happen if we did let people know you were all still here. You'd have television news crews over here within the hour, shoving cameras in your faces and not understanding why you couldn't answer their questions.'

'Television?' Erik stumbled over the unfamiliar word.

'It's too difficult to explain.' Jonathan shrugged. 'Forget I said anything.' He rose to his feet. 'I still have one problem, though, Erik.'

'Whatever it is, you know that I will help you,' Erik replied.

'It's Justine. I can't leave the island without her. I need to get her back from Svein.'

'That will be difficult, I think,' Erik replied. 'He is a stubborn man, and a vindictive one.' His brow creased in thought. 'My father is the man who will know how to resolve this dispute. Let us go and see him now.'

Erik strode off purposefully. Jonathan followed him, wondering what was going through the young Viking's mind. His new ally had reacted with surprising equanimity to the news that his people no longer ruled the world, but it must be hard for him to learn that he and the rest of the men and women on this little island were more isolated than they could have ever believed.

Chapter Nine

Einar stood impassively, arms folded, listening as Erik and Jonathan made their pleas. Jonathan's request was simple: he wanted Svein to release Justine from her slavery.

'This is a difficult thing you ask of me,' Einar replied. 'Under our law, Justine belongs to Svein unless he decides to sell her to someone else. Why should he simply give to these strangers something he has paid for fairly?'

'But surely they have the right to claim her back?' Erik insisted. 'She was their property before she ever came to us.'

Jonathan wondered how Justine would react to the thought of being considered his or Max's property. He glanced across to where she stood on the other side of the room, no doubt trying to gauge how the conversation was progressing from facial expressions and body language alone.

'You know how things are, my son,' Einar said. 'If you had the money, you could simply buy Justine back from Svein. Unfortunately, Jonathan has nothing with which to pay for her, and all the money which you made from selling her has gone to pay the debts you so heedlessly amassed.'

'We could find the money somehow,' Erik said fervently. 'I am sure we could.'

'Even if we did,' Adrienne pointed out, 'there's no

guarantee Svein would sell Justine to us. He might decide to keep her just because he knows how much you want her back.'

'I'm not giving up, Adrienne,' Jonathan replied in English. 'I'll get her from that bastard, whatever it takes.'

'There is a way round this,' Einar said finally. 'The three intruders would have to agree to carry out a test of their endurance. If all three pass, then the girl is free to rejoin her masters. But if one should fail, then she remains in thrall to Svein.'

It was obvious that Adrienne understood what was being asked of them, but Jonathan translated for Max's benefit. His brother shrugged his shoulders. 'Why not? It's not as though we have much of a choice,' he said. 'And anyway, what could they possibly come up with that could be that bad?'

'I don't want to think about that,' Jonathan replied, thinking back to some of the sagas he had studied, and the ferocity of the acts they contained, even from those females who had taken their place on the fields of battle. He looked again at Justine, and knew he had to do whatever he could to save her from a lifetime of slavery at the cruel hands of Svein. He turned to Einar. 'We accept your proposal,' he said.

'Very well.' He appeared to deliberate for a moment, though Jonathan suspected he had already decided what the challenges were to be. 'The first test is to enter the cage of Syn, goddess of trials. Her authority has settled many an argument for us.' Einar smiled, but it was a smile without warmth. 'Whoever agrees to undergo this ordeal must spend three days in the cage without food or water. Only the bravest will attain the favour of the goddess and leave the cage alive. Which of you will accept the

130

challenge?'

Jonathan did not even bother to explain to Max what was required of them. He simply stepped forward and looked Einar straight in the eye. 'I'll do it.'

He was going to die without ever seeing Justine again. Jonathan heaved himself up on to his knees, clutching at the sturdy wooden bars of the cage where he had spent the last sixty hours. Three days and two nights of the worst torment he had ever known. He peered into the distance, trying to focus on the village, his ears straining for any sign of life. But he knew no one would come for at least another twelve hours, and by then it would be too late. This night would be his last on earth.

He had been foolish to think he could succeed in going for so long without water, though he doubted whether Max or Adrienne could have achieved the feat, either. Still, he hadn't hesitated to volunteer, thinking back to his disastrous fall in the Amazon jungle the summer before. Then, it had been almost thirty-six hours before he had been found lying in the bottom of that ravine and flown to safety, and he had survived on the few sips of water remaining at the bottom of the bottle he always carried. Jonathan would have given anything for that bottle now, though he knew it would probably have been torn to shreds by Svein's sharp knife if he had attempted to smuggle it into the cage.

Not that he could have smuggled anything anywhere, dressed as he was in nothing but a strip of coarse material that served to act as a loincloth. Fortunately the cage had a makeshift roof, sheltering him from the worst of the noonday sun, or his skin would have blistered and burned by now, but even the shade could not offer any protection against the fierce, constant thirst that wracked his body.

He flopped back down on the rough earth floor, too weak to do anything else. He had let them down, all of them, and now Justine would be Svein's slave for the rest of her life – unless the man decided to sell her on to someone else who would treat her as a valueless possession. If she had been in thrall to Erik, Jonathan thought he could have borne the pain; that man at least had a kind heart, and had vowed to do all he could in an attempt to keep Justine safe. Even losing Justine to Max would have been preferable, though up till now his brother had proved equally inept at protecting her from the wrath of the Viking warriors. A strangled sound came from Jonathan's parched throat, somewhere between a chuckle and a sob. Max had had to travel halfway across the world to discover that he could not have everything he wanted; Jonathan hoped fervently it would not be the last lesson his brother ever learned.

What would happen to the others, he wondered, when the elders came to this cage in half a day's time and found his lifeless body lying here? Justine's fate was already sealed, and he assumed that Adrienne, too, would be forced to kneel at the feet of a Viking master. But Max? What place was there for Max in this society, where only women served as slaves? Jonathan had the sudden, terrible feeling that he would not be the only one of the Cavendish brothers to die on this Godforsaken island.

'I'm sorry, Max,' he muttered through lips too dry to form the words properly. 'I didn't mean this to happen.' Never mind that his brother had come on this expedition expressly to get his clutches on Justine: Jonathan, as leader of the little party, had had a responsibility to keep the others safe, and he had failed.

I don't want to die, his mind kept repeating. Not here, not now. His body heaved with dry, silent sobs, and his consciousness began to drift.

He had the strangest feeling, as though his soul was rising up from his body, floating effortlessly between the bars of the cage. Suddenly, he was looking down on himself, a motionless figure with buckled limbs and lustreless hair, mouth open as though begging vainly for the water that would have saved his life. The shock was almost enough to send his spirit flooding back to fill that empty vessel, but a stronger force was propelling him onwards.

Jonathan floated over the village. Night was falling and the villagers were preparing for sleep. He saw Erik, tossing wood onto the fire inside his little hut, and Einar, mopping up the last of his evening meal with a hunk of bread. Max was standing at the edge of the circle of huts, staring out in the direction of the clearing where the cage stood. Jonathan would have given anything to know what was going through his brother's mind at that moment. As he watched, Max looked up, shivering as though suddenly cold. He knows I'm here, Jonathan thought. He just can't make the connection.

He moved on, passing the hut where Adrienne slept with one of the village girls. Not that much sleeping appeared to be going on: the lecturer was lying entwined with the young, blonde maiden, sharing secret kisses, their clothes in disarray. Typical Adrienne, taking her pleasure wherever she could find it.

At last he came to Svein's dwelling. The thickset man was nowhere to be seen; only Justine was curled up uncomfortably on a pile of smelly straw, tethered to a peg in the wall by one ankle. Not knowing whether he was awake or hallucinating, Jonathan found himself descending to earth, coming to stand by his girlfriend.

She started at his approach and made to speak, but he motioned her to silence. He gazed at her in the flickering light cast by Svein's meagre fire: wisps of straw were caught in her fair hair; her torn bodice was partly open, revealing the curves of her breasts to him, and her eyes were full of misery and wanting. And yet he could never remember her looking so beautiful.

'Where's Svein?' he whispered.

'He took Gunvor out into the woods,' Justine replied. 'I think they were going to the punishment post. Not that she's done anything to deserve it, of course. The bastard just gets a kick out of it.' She crawled close and reached out to him. 'How did you get here?'

'It doesn't matter,' Jonathan said. 'Anyway, you know it's not your place to ask questions.'

His tone was uncharacteristically harsh, and Justine glanced quizzically at him. 'Are you all right?'

'I told you, no questions,' he repeated. An idea was forming in his mind, coupling with the need that pulsed in his groin. He could feel himself starting to become erect beneath the loose folds of his loincloth. Whatever strength had been sapped from his corporeal body by his ordeal was instantly returned to him a hundredfold. He caught hold of Justine's hair, tangling his fingers in it until her mouth opened to cry out, and pressed his lips down hard on hers in a bruising kiss. Sex with Justine had always been an act of tenderness, but now he felt the urge to be cruel, to draw from her the qualities that made Max want to possess her. Women loved Max because he mastered them, and Jonathan needed to know what that felt like just once before he died.

He pushed Justine away from him, sending her sprawling to the straw. Her lips were red and swollen, and he ached to penetrate them with his cock. He stared down at her, recognising the lack of comprehension in her face.

'Strip,' he ordered, using the icy inflections he remembered from the dinner party where he had first witnessed Max's domination technique. When she hesitated, he grabbed at her bodice, ripping it further. One small breast fell free of the material, and he could see from the way her nipple already stood proud and stiff that her body was excited by the situation even if her mind had not yet come to terms with it.

'Are you going to do as I ask, or do I have to tear the rest off you?' he enquired.

Hurriedly, Justine pulled the dress over her head, throwing it to the floor. She was naked beneath it, and her pussy was still smoothly shaven. The thought of plunging his prick between her denuded labia was producing in Jonathan an erection of almost painful proportions.

He picked up her discarded dress and tore a long strip from the hem. Catching hold of her wrists, he used the piece of material to bind them securely together behind her back.

'On your knees,' he commanded. Awkwardly, Justine rose to her knees, her progress hampered by her tied wrists and the ankle chain that allowed her to move only eighteen inches or so from the wall. Once she was in the required position he stripped off his loincloth.

'Suck it, slut,' he said. 'And do a good job, or I may just have to beat you.' There was no question that Justine would not give him satisfaction; she had always loved to go down on him. As her lips engulfed the tip of his glans and her head began to bob up and down at his crotch, he gave a long, shuddering sigh of delight; the two had not made love since the stopover in New York, which seemed like an incredibly long time ago. However, she seemed intent on giving him a long, leisurely blowjob, in which she set the pace and decided when he was going to come. Max, he decided, would not settle for such treatment. What he would do was exactly what Jonathan did now. He grabbed Justine's blonde hair firmly and held her head still. He began to thrust into her mouth with determined, almost brutal strokes. She made a muffled noise as she struggled to adjust to this change in tempo, and then her throat relaxed and she accepted him.

As soon as he began to feel the spunk roiling in his balls, beginning its ascent of his shaft, he pulled abruptly out of Justine's mouth and pushed her roughly onto her back. Her bound hands were trapped beneath her, and she struggled as he shoved her legs wide apart with the flats of his palms – not with fear did she struggle, he knew, but with mounting excitement. He pushed at her knees until she bent them obediently, opening herself fully for him. Her quim was wet and puffy, the tender tissues swelling with her need. In other circumstances he would have lowered his mouth to taste the delights of her shaven sex, but he was too impatient for release. He ran his cock the length of her crease, holding it for a moment at the entrance to her anus, and watched her eyes widen in shock and expectancy. Erik had trained her to accept this form of penetration, and he knew she would not complain if he followed the Norseman's lead. He noticed she was almost disappointed as he turned his attention instead to her vaginal opening. As he pushed into her with one rough thrust that caused her to cry out at its strength, he began to feel a glimmer of the power that his brother achieved with his sexual domination.

Jonathan thrust in and out with relentless rapidity, feeling Justine's body shudder beneath his as he pressed her down on to the sharp, pricking straw. She was whimpering with every thrust, giving herself up to his will.

Abruptly, he pulled out of her, and she glanced up at him, her eyes registering the loss she felt. Jonathan smiled at her and placed the head of his cock once more at her anal hole. This time he was not teasing: he eased himself into the tight passage, marvelling at the sensation of the ring of muscle that gripped at his shaft. If this was to be the last time he ever came inside Justine's body, let it be in this forbidden way. He sensed that Max would have approved of this decision, and the thought of finally earning his brother's approval was what propelled him into a powerful orgasm. Beneath him he heard Justine making mewling sounds in her throat and realised that she, too, was coming.

He pulled out of her quickly, and rose to his feet. She lay back on the straw, his seed already beginning to ooze out of her anus and down onto her thighs, imploring him to untie her hands. If Svein returned with Gunvor and found Justine naked and bearing all the marks of having received a good fucking, Jonathan dreaded to think what her punishment would be. He bent and unfastened the strip of cloth that bound her wrists.

'Whatever happens, Justine,' he whispered, 'never forget that I love you.' He wanted to say more, but he could feel himself being pulled away from her by the same inexorable force that had led him from the cage of Syn to the village. His last sight of Justine was of her clutching the remnants of her dress to herself, tears of grief beginning to form in her green eyes. He would have given anything to dry those tears, but it seemed that his fate had been decided.

Again he found himself drifting away; his conscious awareness of his surroundings was weakening as the life slowly ebbed from his body. The little settlement receded behind him, and he seemed to rise up into the inky night sky. The air here was cold and wet with the beginning of soft clouds, but there was a light glowing softly in the distance, which brightened as he approached.

He could hear faint sounds: the crackling of a log fire, and singing and shouting in guttural tones. The noise increased in volume as he neared its source, pitching up on suddenly solid ground like a shipwrecked sailor brought to safety on an island shore.

Wearily, Jonathan rose to his feet and stumbled towards what he could now see was a long wooden building. It seemed to stretch infinitely away from him, but he was sure that was just another optical illusion among the many he had experienced in the last few minutes.

A woman stood by the doorway, clutching the bridle of a white horse that pawed the ground restlessly. She was tall, easily Jonathan's height, and lightly clad in silvery armour. The breastplate she wore seemed only to enhance the swelling of her magnificent breasts, and her long, slender legs were bare beneath a skirt of far finer material than that worn by any of the village women. Her white-blonde hair hung loose to her waist, and a fearsome-looking axe hung from the belt that cinched her tiny waist. She smiled as Jonathan approached.

'Welcome, brave warrior,' she said in a low, melodious voice. 'There is a place at the table for you.'

As she pushed aside the heavy wooden door, he realised where he was. Valhalla, final resting place of those slain in battle. Within its palatial walls the heroes feasted with Odin, eating meat from a sacred boar that was slain and cooked each evening, only to return to life the following morning, and drinking mead from Odin's sacred goat. Every morning they would ride out and fight with each other, inflicting the most terrible wounds, and every night those wounds would heal, tended by the Valkyrie maidens. It was hardly Jonathan's idea of heaven.

Another woman, almost the twin of the first, caught his arm as he stepped into the hall, his eyes blinking fiercely as they tried to adjust to the dimly lit, smoky atmosphere. The perspective in the room seemed wrong, somehow, and no matter how hard he tried, he could not see to the far wall. The smell of roasting meat filled his nostrils, making his mouth water. All around him men were laughing and shouting, eating greedily from plates piled high with boar's flesh and gulping mead from iron goblets.

He was led to a gap on one of the long wooden benches, and the Valkyrie bade him sit. His companions at the table eyed him with curiosity, and he was suddenly uncomfortably aware of his naked state. Those around him were dressed for battle, and their bodies seemed to be in different states of repair. Some bore gaping wounds, and he was certain that, further down the table, he could see one man whose arm hung almost severed from its shoulder, and another who had the helm of an axe buried deep in his skull. Closer to him were others whose flesh was healing, knitting itself back together with scar tissue that gleamed pinkly in the candlelight. Others appeared unscathed, the regeneration process complete. Jonathan shook his head, trying to make sense of what he saw.

Valkyries flitted between the tables, refilling plates and jugs, and stroking their delicate hands along the limbs and cheeks of the feasting warriors. They were of a uniform, ethereal beauty, which Jonathan was sure he would have appreciated more had he not been so weary and undernourished.

He hoped that he would be allowed to eat and drink, but no food was set before him. Instead, a low, almost hypnotic music began to play, like nothing he had ever heard.

This seemed to be the pre-arranged signal for some form of entertainment. A girl stepped into the wide rectangle of floor space between the tables. She was the most stunning of all the women in this place, her hair so pale it seemed to have no colour, but reflected the flickering light of the fire, her skin smooth and unblemished and her eyes the clear blue of an early-morning sky. Unlike the other Valkyries, she wore no armour, and her dress was of gauzy, insubstantial stuff that did nothing to hide the full, high globes of her breasts, crowned with the palest pink areolae, or the wisp of fair hair that covered her pubic delta.

The music increased in tempo, very slightly. Jonathan looked round for the musicians who were producing it. To the cheers of the watching heroes, the girl began to dance. Her movements were sinuous, her arms weaving patterns in the smoky air of the hut as her hips gyrated in a figure of eight. This was a dance intended to arouse and excite, and as he watched, Jonathan felt his cock beginning to rise again.

His attention entirely concentrated on the dancer, he did not at first notice two of the Valkyries hauling something into the centre of the floor. That something, he gradually realised, was a wooden frame bearing in its centre a St Andrew's cross – not that any of these warriors would have known who St Andrew was, Jonathan thought.

The two Valkyries glanced at each other, and then, in a choreographed movement, surrounded the dancing girl and caught hold of her by the wrists. Though she was making attempts to pull away from them, it was obvious that this was all part of the performance. They dragged her over to the frame, and swiftly tethered her wrists and ankles to the extremities of the cross, spread-eagling her. The watching Viking warriors had fallen silent, and Jonathan realised they all knew what was about to happen.

One of the Valkyries who had tied the girl to the cross stepped forward and spoke, her voice as soft and sweet as that of her sister who stood at the entrance to this hall. 'It is time for the punishment to commence,' she said, her words greeted by a mighty cheer. 'As always, one of you will be chosen to enact the ritual, and as we have a newcomer in our midst, so the task will fall to him.'

She walked over to Jonathan and held out a hand. 'Come, prove your worth.'

Awkwardly, Jonathan rose to his feet, uncertain of what was expected of him. He had never punished anyone in his life and here, in this mythical feasting hall, surrounded by an army of dead warriors, did not seem the best place to begin.

He stood close to the whipping frame. The willowy blonde who was fastened so securely in place in the centre of the frame turned her head to look at him. He had never seen a face quite so heartbreakingly beautiful. Her pale blue eyes held a depth of experience he could not begin to guess at, their world-weary depths totally at odds with the innocent perfection of her features and girlish body.

He felt as though she was staring right into his soul, taking the measure of him. He wondered what exactly she would make of what she saw there.

The Valkyrie maiden who had called Jonathan to perform the punishment now began to unfasten the belt that bound her dress, and as she did so he realised it was actually an intricately fashioned whip, thicker and heavier than the one which Svein had used on Justine. She handed it to Jonathan, who tried to take it with an air of insouciance, as though he was not a novice in these matters. He sensed that his performance was not fooling his intended victim.

Without a word, the second Valkyrie took hold of the suspended girl's gauzy dress, and ripped it apart with one swift tug, leaving her back and buttocks exposed to the watching audience. Like her face, her body was exquisite, the pale skin utterly unblemished. Jonathan blanched at the thought of marring that perfection with the whip, but he knew she was not unwilling. Perhaps she was like the warriors, he thought. Every night her body was whipped and abused, and every day it slowly regenerated until it was perfect once more and ready for more punishment.

He hefted the whip experimentally, trying to accustom himself to its alien weight and feel. There was an impatient murmuring from the feasting Vikings, who were anxious for the show to begin. Jonathan positioned himself slightly to the side of the girl, remembering how Svein had stood by Justine when he had been beating her.

At last, he swung the whip, watching as it sliced through the air and landed on the girl's back. The blow was not hard enough to do more than redden her skin slightly, and there was a groan of disappointment, both from those who were watching, and, Jonathan was convinced, from the girl herself.

This time he put more power into his wrist action, and the whip fell with a vengeance. A long, pronounced weal sprang up on her porcelain flesh, and she gave an agonised moan. That had hurt. That was what they wanted to see.

Gaining confidence with every stroke, Jonathan began to lay parallel stripes down the length of her back and down to her taut, round buttocks. Lacking the ease and familiarity with which Svein had handled the whip, he found it almost impossible to prevent it from falling on weals he had already laid. Though the skin was not broken, it was criss-crossed with angry red and purple marks. Occasionally, the very tip of the whip would curl round the girl's body, the well-used leather cutting into the soft flesh of her small, high breasts or inner thighs. Then she would give out a high-pitched shriek, unable to disguise the pain she was feeling, and the spectral warriors would respond with lusty cheers.

Jonathan glanced round, and saw that his performance was having the intended effect on its audience. Many of the Vikings had pulled un-protesting Valkyries on to their laps, and were kissing and caressing them. More than one of the women was sitting with her armour removed and her breasts exposed for her partner to stroke or suckle on, while her hands were busy in his lap, fondling his prick. Jonathan, too, was experiencing the same feelings of arousal as he had when watching Justine being whipped, though now he was the one who was actually inflicting the punishment, the sensation was even more pronounced. He had forgotten he was naked, and that his almost painfully erect cock was on display to everyone in the hall; it would have been nice, he thought, if one of the Valkyries would take him in hand, and play with his erection until he came, but he knew that his chosen woman was the one whose body he had been tormenting so cruelly with the whip.

His arm had fallen still as he surveyed the scenes of debauchery around him. To his surprise, the girl turned her head and stared at him with eyes full of need and desire. 'Don't stop,' she begged. 'Whip me again, Master.'

The unfamiliar word on her soft lips was all it took to spur Jonathan into action once more. Again he brought the whip down on her back, striping her flesh with the marks she craved. She was screaming and thrashing in her bonds, trying to ride the waves of suffering as they engulfed her. Jonathan was amazed to see a tell tale trace of silvery juice running down the inside of her thigh. Her mind was translating the pain into pleasure, her body lubricating itself in readiness for sex.

He threw the whip down and went to stand right behind her, using the weight of his body to pinion her tighter to the wooden cross. He pulled the last, tattered remnants of her dress from around her waist, seeking to discover exactly what he had done to her. His fingers traced the marks of the whip down her sides and over the swell of her breasts, and when she moaned under his touch, it was with longing. Her sex was at the perfect height for him to enter as he stood there; peeling her nether lips apart he inserted his cock into her moist channel with a thrust hard enough to drive the breath from her.

For the second time in the space of a few hours, his manhood was buried deep in the secret, welcoming heart of a woman's body. Unlike Justine's hot quim, however, this girl's vagina was surprisingly cool, as though Jonathan had plunged his shaft into cream fresh from the fridge. The sensation did not make his erection shrivel, as he might have expected; instead, he found himself growing longer and harder. She was sighing and gasping beneath him, her pubic bone pressed hard against the wood and receiving stimulation every time he powered into her.

He could have stayed in that strange, cold fleshy embrace forever. Having already come with Justine, he knew that this time he would last longer, and so it proved. Minutes passed while he thrust into the girl, only vaguely aware that, all around him, the Viking warriors were imitating his actions, coupling with the Valkyrie maidens.

At last Jonathan's hips gave a convulsive spasm, and his cock spat its seed into the girl's sex. He slumped against her body, the whipping frame supporting both of them as they fought for their breath. Eventually he stepped away, and unfastened her wrists and ankles. She collapsed onto him, clutching tight to his arms and whispered in his ear.

'You should know my true identity now, stranger,' she told him. 'I am no simple dancing girl. I am Syn, goddess of trials.'

'What?' Jonathan exclaimed. 'But I – I whipped you. And you enjoyed it.'

'Why does that surprise you?'

'I'm sorry,' Jonathan said. 'Forgive me, goddess. I didn't mean to hurt you.'

'If there was hurt, then I wanted it,' she murmured. 'You have done well, stranger.'

One of the Valkyries handed her an iron cup, which she scarcely had the strength to hold. 'You have passed your trial, and you have my blessing. Come, drink of the mead of Heidrun. It will restore you.'

She pressed the cup to Jonathan's lips, and he gulped greedily at it. It was strong, sweet and potent, like nothing else he had ever drunk, and he felt the strength beginning to return to his exhausted limbs. Again he felt the strange disconnection from his body which had started his journey here, and Syn's hold on him became less substantial. He closed his eyes, and let himself drift away.

'He's still alive!'

The voice was familiar, but Jonathan could not place it. It seemed to be coming from a vast distance away, and he struggled towards it like a swimmer rising towards the surface of the sea.

He opened his eyes to see a face staring down at him. A beautiful face with skin the colour of caramel and wide, dark eyes that seemed to brim with tears. The knowledge of who she was flooded back to him, and he spoke her name. 'Adrienne.'

'Thank God,' she whispered.

Another face joined hers. Max, his brother, lines of worry etched on his handsome face. 'Jon, I can't believe it. We saw you lying there, and we thought…'

'Don't worry.' The words came out as little more than a croak. 'I'm fine.'

'Don't try to speak,' Max urged him. 'We'll get you some water to drink. You must be more than ready for some.'

Jonathan shook his head, weakly. 'That's the odd thing. I'm not thirsty at all. It was Syn, she—' He fell silent, thinking back to the beautiful goddess who had used the sacred mead of the gods to quench his thirst, and wondered if either Max or Adrienne had noticed that, although he had been without water in this little cage for three days, his lips were lightly beaded with drops of moisture.

Chapter Ten

Justine was fast asleep and dreaming. In her mind she was employed as Max's secretary at Cavendish Publications, having accepted his offer of work experience during the long summer vacation. He had asked her to make him a cup of coffee, and she had gone into the little kitchen used by the editorial staff, boiled the kettle, poured hot water over the coffee grounds, and waited for it to brew. She had filled a mug, adding milk and sugar before taking it into Max's office.

He looked up from his paperwork and acknowledged her briefly. She turned to leave the office as Max took a sip of his coffee. 'Justine,' he said sharply, and she looked round to see a grimace of distaste on his face. 'You've put sugar in this coffee, haven't you? How many times have I told you?'

She put a hand to her head. 'Oh, Max, I'm so sorry. I'm so used to Jonathan taking sugar in his coffee, I completely forgot.'

'It's just not good enough, I'm afraid, Justine.' Max sighed, twisting his elegant silver fountain pen between his long fingers. 'I was hoping to send you away from here with a glowing reference, but when you make such a simple mistake, the only thing you'll be leaving with is a glowing backside.'

Justine swallowed as the implications of his words sank in. 'You wouldn't…'

'Oh, you know perfectly well I would, Justine. You continue to confuse me with my brother, and you have to be taught that we're completely different. It seems the only way I'm going to be able to teach you that is by drilling it into you by hand, if you see what I mean.' He smiled, pleased with his pun, picked up his phone and dialled a number. 'Alan, would you come into my office for a moment? And bring Simon with you.'

Alan Parkin was Max's deputy editor, and Simon Moore the office junior, at seventeen a couple of years younger than Justine. Within seconds they were both standing in Max's office. Justine looked at the pair of them with a sinking heart; she had no idea whether the short, dark-haired Alan or the gangly, fair-haired Simon had any knowledge of their employer's sadistic tendencies, but she was sure they were about to find out.

Max rose from his chair and settled himself on the edge of his desk, facing the two men. 'This will only take a few minutes,' he said. 'I'm having a bit of a problem with Justine here, and I'm afraid I'm going to have to instil a little discipline into her, to make sure she remembers what she's told in future. I thought having the pair of you here to watch the proceedings might help reinforce the message.'

Justine knew that whatever Max intended to do to her, having Alan and Simon present would really serve to increase the level of humiliation she would feel at being punished.

'Justine, would you fetch my chair, please?'

Max could quite easily have walked round his desk and picked up the chair himself, but he wanted to remind her of her lowly place in this hierarchy. She scurried round and placed the heavy, armless wooden chair on the bare expanse of carpet in front of Max's desk. He went to sit down on it, taking his time to make himself comfortable and adjust the lie of his trousers. The dark woollen material seemed baggy around his crotch, but Justine knew that soon his erection would be tenting it out.

'Over my knee, please, Justine,' he said.

'I... I can't,' Justine said. 'Max, please don't make me do this.'

'Do I have to ask Alan or Simon to put you there?' Max asked.

Justine glanced at the two newcomers. Alan Parkin was leaning against the wall, arms folded, a strange look of anticipation on his face, and she knew in that moment that this was a scene he had witnessed in the past. Simon, on the other hand, was staring at her wide-eyed, not quite able to believe what was happening. She had no intention of letting either of them get involved in the proceedings and so, reluctantly, she climbed onto Max's lap, face down, her fingers and toes stretching to reach the pile of the deep blue office carpet.

The neat black skirt she was wearing was stretched taut across her backside, and Max smoothed his hand over the material for a moment before making a decision. 'Raise your skirt, please, Justine,' he said.

She thought about protesting, but realised that if she did he would only invite one of the others to perform the chore. Slowly and carefully, she reached behind and eased the tight material up over her thighs and bottom while Max held her steady on his lap. Once she had done this he tucked the hem of her skirt into the waistband, so it would not come loose as he spanked her. Now her pink cotton panties were on view to all the men in the room; the gusset had ridden up slightly into the cleft between her legs, and she could feel her cheeks colouring in shame.

'Very nice,' Max muttered absently, stroking his hand over her backside again. Suddenly, and without warning, the stroke became a slap, her flesh reverberating under the force of the unexpected blow. She winced and wriggled against his muscular thighs.

'Keep still, Justine,' he warned in a low voice, and brought his hand down once more. The blow stung, but this time she did her best not to react to it.

Slowly and methodically Max gave her a dozen slaps, alternating on each buttock, but varying the space between them so that she never knew when the next one would fall. The blows were not particularly hard, but they had set up a dull, throbbing ache beneath the skin. She kept her eyes firmly fixed to the floor throughout, afraid that if she looked up she would meet the gaze of Alan or Simon. She had no idea how they were reacting to the sight of her being chastised by Max, but she suspected their reaction was not dissimilar to his own. As she had predicted, his cock was now a thick, solid bar of flesh against which her pubis was pressing.

He sat back in his chair, and she thought the punishment was over. She had managed to take all twelve slaps without crying out or moving on Max's lap, and she was inwardly pleased with herself. Her inward air of self-satisfaction disappeared at his next words.

'So that's twelve for putting sugar in my coffee. Now for another twelve for confusing me with that egghead brother of mine. As that's the more grievous error it deserves a more serious punishment, so we'll have these on the bare. Take your knickers off, Justine.'

'No... please...' There was no way Justine could bare her bottom before two men who she hardly knew. They had already witnessed her take a spanking over her semi-clad backside, seen how the subtle pain was beginning to make her outer labia swell around the edges of the gusset of her panties, but she could not take the final step and let them see her most intimate places.

'Very well, then,' Max said. 'Alan, would you do the honours?'

Justine tried to jump up from Max's lap, but he held her in a tight grip. Vainly, she kicked her legs and struggled as the deputy editor firmly and swiftly stripped the little panties from her.

'Nice, aren't they?' Max said to Alan. 'Keep them as a souvenir.'

Now there was nothing Justine could do to shield herself. Max began to spank her again, harder this time, and when she began to squirm and try to move away from his hand he did nothing to prevent her. She knew this was because the movements would reveal more of her sex to Alan and Simon, but the slaps were too painful for her to bear stoically and in stillness. There was silence in the room, punctuated only by the echoing noise of Max's hand buffeting against her arse cheeks. They were only twelve slaps, but as pain mounted on pain they felt more like a hundred. Her bottom was burning, and so was her pussy. She could feel the white heat of submissive yearning deep in her womb, stimulated by her chastisement and the humiliation she felt at receiving it, and she could not stop herself wishing that Max would slide down the zip on his trousers and plunge his hugely erect cock deep into her moist channel.

'So have you learned anything this afternoon, Justine?' Max was asking.

'Yes, Max,' she replied contritely. 'You don't take sugar

in your coffee, and you're not Jonathan.'

'Very good, Justine,' Max said, 'but I don't think you're the only one who's learned some valuable lessons. I think Simon may have picked up a thing or two from what's been going on. Isn't that right, Simon?'

'Er… yes, Mr Cavendish,' Simon replied. Justine glanced across to see that the boy's dark trousers were straining to contain an impressive-looking bulge, and the pupils of his hazel eyes were large and dark with desire. 'I'm going to have to be very careful if I make coffee for you in future.'

'That wasn't quite what I meant,' Max said. 'You may be thinking that this is no way to treat one of your employees, but you see, Justine is no ordinary employee. There are many women who would react with anger and disgust if I tried to punish them the way I've punished Justine, and would slap a suit for sexual harassment on me. However, for all her indignation, Justine actually enjoyed what I've just done to her, and I can prove it to you. Come here, Simon.'

Justine held her breath as the boy approached. She had thought that Max was about to call a halt to her ordeal, but this was not the case. Simon stood close to her, looking down on her fiery red backside, mottled with the marks of Max's palm.

'Now, I don't know how much experience you've had with the opposite sex, Simon,' Max said, hauling Justine into a sitting position and catching hold of her wrists, 'but I'm sure you know there are some obvious ways to tell whether or not a woman is turned on. One is that her nipples become erect. Do you want to see whether that's the case with Justine? Go ahead, feel them and find out. Justine won't mind.'

Justine, mute with embarrassment, was all too aware that she did not mind. Her nipples were pushing against the heavy white cotton of her blouse, and she was desperate to feel someone's fingers stroking and teasing them. She was aware of the slight sting of her flesh where it rubbed on Max's woollen trousers, and the bulk of his erection wedged against her bottom. Simon reached out and, a little clumsily, ran his hands down the front of her blouse. She felt her nipples peaking even further at his tentative touch and moaned softly, wanting him to caress them more roughly.

'Take a look at them, Simon,' Max urged. 'See how stiff they are.'

Simon, hardly believing what he was being told to do, unbuttoned Justine's blouse with fumbling fingers. With Max holding her wrists, she was unable to prevent Simon pulling the blouse out of the waistband of her skirt and opening it wide to show her pert breasts to Alan. Now he did cup them and touch her nipples with more force, twisting them till she cried out with the intensely erotic pain.

'Go easy, Simon,' Max said. 'We don't want her enjoying herself too much, do we?'

Justine twisted in his grasp, but could not break free. She longed to wipe the arrogant smile from Max Cavendish's face, but, despite herself, she longed to give herself to him even more.

'So the nipples are erect,' Max continued with the detached tone of a man conducting a scientific study, 'but if a woman is really turned on her juices will be flowing freely; ready to ease the passage of a man's cock into her body. Simon, would you do the honours?'

Justine had been keeping her knees together, trying to

hide as much of her vulva from the men's gaze as she could, but now Simon, gaining in confidence with every moment, prised them apart. She knew he would see that her sex was open and ready, glistening with her own lubrication.

He did not need Max to tell him to reach out and touch the slippery folds of flesh. His index finger gently began to probe and explore, running over her sensitive lips before finally settling on the hard little nub of her clitoris.

'That's it,' Max whispered. 'Touch her there, Simon. Make her come. See what a wanton little slut she is.' Simon's finger moved faster and faster over her clit, bringing her ever closer to the orgasm she craved. A second finger slipped into her vagina, as far as it would go. Her head swimming with pleasure, she was vaguely aware that Max had let go of her wrists and was unzipping his trousers, loosing his cock in readiness to fuck her. She had the certainty that in this perverse mood he would not choose the usual orifice in which to insert it, and the thought of the animalistic coupling to come forced her over the edge into a gasping climax that went on and on...

She woke with a start to find herself lying on the floor of Svein's hut, her thighs damp with the excitement the dream had caused. Of course Max was on her mind, with the thought of his impending ordeal to come, but why did she have to dream about him in such an explicit fashion? It should be Jonathan who was the focus of her thoughts, she told herself angrily, but it seemed that, even mentally, it was Max who was providing the dominance she sought. Though after the strange visitation she had experienced on the last night of Jonathan's ordeal, which she was increasingly convinced had not been a dream, she was beginning to suspect that her boyfriend was learning a few tricks from his elder sibling.

Svein grunted and stirred in his sleep, and Justine realised it would soon be dawn. Almost time, she thought, to learn exactly what Max would have to do as part of the attempt to free her from her unwanted slavery.

Again, Max, Jonathan and Adrienne stood before Einar, awaiting the elder's pronouncement. It seemed that one or two of the villagers who had originally shown hostility to the strangers were now treating Jonathan with a new respect: no one had expected him to pass the ordeal in the cage of Syn, but he stood before them now, still a little weak and dehydrated, but healthy enough considering he had gone for so many hours without food and water.

Max glanced at his brother, wondering if he would ever get to the bottom of what had happened over the course of those hours. Jonathan had not wanted to talk about it, not even to him. When they had pulled him from the cage, delirious, he had been mumbling something about the protection of the goddess, but once he had recovered something like his old composure, he had denied all knowledge of any such words. Max put it out of his mind, more concerned with what his own trial would comprise. It had been decided in advance that he would take the next ordeal, to give Einar time to think of something that was best suited to him.

At last Einar spoke, and Max waited for Jonathan to translate his words. 'I know that of all of you, you are the one who considers himself to be the master, able to make any woman bend to his will. Well, we have a woman among us who bends to no man. She has the strength of a warrior, and the same fearsome determination. Your task is to defeat her in three trials of strength. You must swim further, shoot an arrow a greater distance and finally wrestle her into submission. If you fail in any of these trials, Justine remains with Svein.'

'Who is this woman?' Max asked.

'Step forward, Hilde.' Einar beckoned to a young woman standing close by. Max gasped in disbelief as she approached. She was easily his own height, and the simple dress she wore did little to disguise a bulky figure which, Max quickly realised, consisted of muscle rather than fat. Her breasts were enormous, straining the woollen fabric of her dress, her hips wide and her legs long and strong. She seemed to Max like one of the operatic sopranos who would take the role of Brunnhilde in a performance of Wagner's Ring cycle, or some silicon-enhanced adventuress from a sword and sorcery film, but this was no parody of a Valkyrie maiden: this was the real thing.

'I've got to beat her?' he muttered to Jonathan.

'Well, as Einar said, you are the great master,' Jonathan replied. 'Just pretend she's one of my girlfriends. You can usually get them to do anything you want.'

Max was too stung by his brother's words to reply. Eventually he turned to Adrienne and said, 'Tell Einar I accept, but if that brother of mine thinks I'm doing this to help him, then he's mistaken. This is for Justine, and no one else.'

Half an hour later they stood on the rocky shore, close to where the light aircraft had dropped Jonathan and his party. The sea was calmer today, stretching out to the horizon as an unruffled sheet of blue-grey. Unlike Jonathan, Max was not intended to undergo his ordeal in solitude: most of the men in the village had turned out to watch him take on Hilde, and Svein was also there, Justine huddled in her chains by his side. No doubt the silversmith hoped he would fail; with these odds, Max thought there was more than a fair chance of that happening.

At Einar's next instruction Max realised why so many of the men were crowding around Hilde; both he and she were expected to go naked. Quickly Max stripped off his shirt, jeans and underwear, aware that all eyes were turned to Hilde as she disrobed. Naked, she was, if anything, an even more impressive sight: the strength of her pectoral muscles meant that her large breasts barely sagged under their own weight, her belly was surprisingly flat, and her thigh muscles were as finely sculpted as those of any world-class sprinter. Max wondered how she had come to be so well-honed, given that the people of Odinland had turned their back on physical conquest centuries ago, but then he reckoned that if Hilde wanted to remain a free woman in a society that had enslaved all her sisters, the strength to beat any man in a fight was probably a necessary asset. He found himself shivering despite the heat of the day, and glanced over towards Justine for reassurance. She smiled at him, uncertainly, no doubt afraid that Svein was watching her, but, like all the other men, his attention seemed riveted to Hilde's statuesque form.

Max and Hilde stood side by side at the edge of the water. The warrior woman gave him a look of contempt that made his cock shrivel. She seemed not to care that Justin's freedom was ultimately the prize in this battle; she simply wanted to have the satisfaction of beating yet another man on her own terms. So much for female solidarity, Max thought.

'On my signal, you will swim to the rock you can see

standing by itself at the far entrance to this cove. The one who rounds it and returns to the shore first will be the winner of this part of the contest.' He paused while Jonathan explained to Max what was requested of him, then raised his hand above his head. The watching crowd fell silent as he dropped his arm to his side, and Max and Hilde plunged into the waves.

Max had always been a strong swimmer, and even in this unfamiliar stretch of water he felt he had a good chance of competing with Hilde on even terms. The rock Einar had indicated was about a mile from the shore, and he struck out towards it in a smooth front crawl. Pacing himself so he would not tire too soon, he kept up easily with Hilde, but as they began to near the weathered finger of limestone that pointed upwards from the waves, he sensed her pulling away from him. Soon she was several metres ahead, her long hair trailing behind her like golden seaweed.

The sea was more choppy around the rock, slowing the progress of both swimmers, and a couple of times Max found a wave slapping him in the face, leaving him to splutter out a mouthful of salt water. Undaunted, he pressed on, turning in a smooth, neat semi-circle and beginning the return journey to the shore. Hilde was still ahead of him, but her movements were not so fluid now, her kicking feet throwing up little plumes of foam. She had tried to put too much distance between herself and Max, and now she was paying the price. As they drew nearer to the little group standing waiting on the shore, Max realised that Hilde could only be a metre or so ahead of him, and she was visibly tiring. Summoning his reserves of energy, he kicked out and closed on her further. She turned her head and glared at him, but she had no other answer. When the two of them finally staggered to the shore, the length of Max's fingers separated them.

They lay there, gasping, on the cool, damp sand, as Einar looked down on them. 'I declare the stranger to be the winner,' he said, shaking his head as though he had expected another result.

They headed back up the beach. The second test of their strength was shooting at a target. Einar handed both of them a bow and a selection of flint-tipped arrows. Hilde quickly fitted an arrow to her bow, raised it and gazed down past the bowstring impassively. Max took his own bow as though it were red-hot, and stared helplessly at it.

'I didn't think the Vikings were into bows and arrows,' Max said to Jonathan. 'I thought if they were out hunting their prey, they preferred to hack lumps off it with a sword, or hold it down and bite its head off with their teeth.'

'You've got such an original grasp of history,' Jonathan retorted.

'We call it gallows humour where I come from,' Adrienne observed.

'Is it that obvious that I'm petrified?' Max asked. 'I've never used one of these things in my life.'

'Well, you'll have three attempts to match Hilde, according to Einar,' Jonathan told him. 'The target is that tree stump over there. Whoever gets closest to hitting it is the winner.'

'Can I go and say goodbye to Justine now?' Max asked.

'You're not giving up yet, are you?' Jonathan asked. 'I thought you were more of a man than that.'

Max said nothing, but Jonathan's words had had the intended effect of galvanising him into action. He raised the bow and slotted an arrow into the notch at the centre of its smooth curve, as Hilde had done. She was to have the honour of shooting first, and he watched as she loosed the arrow. It flew in a powerful arc, coming to rest within ten metres of the specified tree stump. There were low mutters from those who were watching; it had been a good shot, and they doubted that Max's effort would beat it.

They were right. Although Max did his best to copy Hilde's actions, the unfamiliar weight and motion of the bow as he loosed the arrow unsettled him, and the arrow came to land less than halfway to the stump.

Again Hilde aimed and fired, and though this shot was not so powerful, she did not seem unduly worried. When Max's second shot once more fell short of her first effort – though it was much closer than his previous attempt had been – she allowed a contemptuous smile to cross her face.

'I shall forego my third shot,' she announced, the tone of her voice clearly stating that she had already won the competition.

Spurred on by her arrogance, Max raised the bow for the third and final time. He paused for a moment, searching his mental and physical resources for the strength to succeed. Goddess, whoever you are, he begged in a silent prayer; you helped Jonathan, now please help me. I can't bear to lose Justine to that bastard Svein.

He closed his eyes and loosed his shot, turning away before it had even fallen so as not to witness the evidence of his own failure.

There was a gasp from the collected onlookers, and he spun on his heel. His prayer had been answered. The arrow had fallen a centimetre or two closer to the tree stump than Hilde's best effort.

She was looking at him as though she could not comprehend what had happened. Max could scarcely believe it himself. Still, she had chosen to forfeit her final shot; she could not change her mind now.

'Again, the stranger is the winner,' Einar said. 'Only the wrestling remains now.'

A circle had been marked out on the hard, sandy earth close to where the target shooting had taken place.

'The winner of this contest will be the one who makes the other submit,' Einar declared. 'To make things more interesting, the two competitors will have their bodies oiled first.'

Seemingly from nowhere, two pots of sweet-smelling unguent were produced. Adrienne was ordered to rub it over Max's skin, while Jonathan did the same for Hilde. Max found the combination of Adrienne's fingers smoothing the oily potion into his body and the sight of Jonathan working it into Hilde's firm, muscular form almost unbearably arousing, and his cock began to rise from the mat of fair hair at his groin. He was aware of Hilde's gaze on his swelling penis, and the sheer curiosity in her eyes made him wonder whether she had ever seen a man's erection before. If she was sworn to live a life that kept her free from slavery, it was entirely possible that she was still a virgin, he reasoned.

At last, Adrienne stepped away from him. His flesh glistened with the sweet unguent, and he ran an experimental finger over his chest, feeling its slipperiness. It would be hard for either wrestler to get a purchase on the other's body, which would prolong the bout for the spectators.

Max and Hilde stepped into the roughly drawn ring and faced each other. Max's heart pounded in his chest as he waited for Einar to give the signal that the contest was to begin. When it came, Hilde lunged at him, seeking to catch hold of his arms; her fingers scrabbled on his oily skin as he managed to side step her. She turned and rushed towards him again; they tangled with each other, and Hilde used her foot to trip Max, sending him sprawling to the earth. She tried to flop down onto his prone body, but he rolled to one side and she landed heavily, winded. He caught a fistful of her long hair and she shook her head back and forth vigorously, attempting to free herself. They rolled over and over on the ground, naked and sweating, their sides heaving and their faces contorted with the sheer effort of fighting.

Hilde was on top of Max now, her heavy body pressing his own into the ground. She was determined to be the winner in this bout, and Max gave a yelp as her sharp white teeth closed sharply on his earlobe.

'You little bitch,' he exclaimed, even though he knew she could not understand him. 'If that's the way you want to play it…'

He wriggled down beneath her body so that his head was level with her breasts, and took one of her nipples in his mouth. A wicked smile crossed his face as he bit down on the tender bud; not hard enough to damage her, but she registered the sudden pain with a gasp of shock.

There were shouts of encouragement from the onlookers, who liked the way this fight was developing. Max suspected that, even though he was the outsider and thus the one who was intended to lose, there was more than one man here who had sought to master Hilde, and who was willing Max to succeed where he had failed. They wanted this haughty, wild woman to be put in her place, and a groundswell of support was building for the blond Englishman.

Hilde's powerful thighs clasped around Max's back, seeking to squeeze the breath from him. He gasped as he felt the pressure increasing on his ribcage; wondered how much it would take for her to crack a bone or two. His hands clawed at her breasts, and the tension on his ribs lessened almost imperceptibly as a sound suspiciously like a sigh escaped from Hilde's lips.

'This is turning you on, you bitch,' Max gasped, and in that moment he realised he had the power to defeat her. The knowledge gave him the extra burst of strength he needed. Finally managing to free her thighs from around his body, he pushed her back onto the ground and watched as she lay panting, her legs still widely spread. Droplets of moisture were visible on her soft blonde pubic hair; a mixture, Max suspected, not just of sweat and the lubricating unguent, but also of her own feminine excitement.

He knelt over her, his body straddling hers so that the tip of his erect cock was just touching the folds of her labia. Her hands came up, reaching for his windpipe, but the fight had gone from her eyes. Max caught her by the wrists and pushed her hands flat to the ground. Inching up her body, he presented his erection to her lips, knowing the risk he was taking. She could simply open her mouth, close those strong white teeth around his glans, and bite…

He prepared himself for the worst. What he felt was a curious tongue, reaching out to lick the taut purple crown, already pulling away from the velvet sheath of skin that contained it. He shuddered as her lips closed around his cock head and began to suck. The watching crowd had fallen silent; this was not the outcome they had been expecting. Max closed his eyes, oblivious to everything but the wet pressure of Hilde's mouth on his shaft. She was beginning to bend to his will; once he had mastered her completely he would have passed the ordeal, and Justine would be another step closer to her freedom.

Inexperienced as she was, Hilde was doing just enough to propel him towards his climax, and his eyes fluttered open with the realisation that he was closer to coming than he had intended.

He pulled sharply out of her mouth, leaving her to stare at him with puzzlement. Again he slid down her body, settling his cock at the entrance to her sex once more. She lay prone, her breasts rising and falling as her breathing quickened in anticipation. He used his fingers to gently peel apart her large, ragged inner lips, revealing the tight, dark channel beneath them. With infinite slowness he eased the first half-inch or so of his prick into that channel, feeling it cede gradually to his passage. Soon he came to the thin membrane that still bore witness to her virgin state. He wanted to reassure her that what he was about to do was not intended to hurt her, but he could not make himself understood. Instead, he thrust in hard, feeling that last barrier break under the force. She cried out; it was a wild, keening sound, pain and accusation shining in her eyes. But as he kept on thrusting the pain gave way to pleasure, and when she called out again there was a different tone to the sound, something almost feral, like a wild cat in the throes of mating.

Max kept up a steady rhythm, taking delight in the way Hilde had begun to respond. His hands stroked over her firm, sweat-dampened breasts, and her legs came up to clasp round his back once more, but this time there was no aggression in the gesture.

Their bodies rocked and juddered together as Max's

movements became more spasmodic and he surrendered to the inevitable outpouring of his climax. He lay still for a moment before pulling out, aware that Hilde had not come, but too worn out from the exertions of his ordeal to have tried to pace his orgasm to match her own. As he watched, she brought her own finger down to touch her clitoris. Max went to slap her hand away, wanting to enjoy the task himself. The blow fell on the flesh of her inner thigh. Hilde sighed, and rubbed her clit faster.

Inspired by the sight, Max pushed her over onto her stomach, trapping her busily working hand beneath her. Her buttocks were hard and muscular, as opposed to the softer cheeks of the women he usually punished, but they were no less tempting for that. His palm fell in a rapid blur, judiciously peppering those buttocks and the very tops of her thighs. Hilde was yelling, the sound throaty and uninhibited, and she was squirming on her own fingers. It took no more than a few seconds before she was arching her back and curling her toes and fingers with the strength of the sensations flooding through her. The moment of her orgasm went on and on, and then she flopped back on the hard ground, exhausted.

Max was suddenly aware of Einar and Jonathan standing beside him. He propped himself up wearily on one elbow, conscious of his tired, dirty state and his cock resting limp and flaccid on his thigh.

'Einar tells me that you've passed your ordeal,' Jonathan said, squatting down beside him. The two brothers embraced awkwardly, sensing that a new bond had been formed between them. Both had been taken to their mental and physical limits in their attempts to help Justine, and each had to respect the other for having succeeded. 'However,' he continued, 'there is the small matter of what you're going to do with your new slave.'

'Slave?' Max queried.

'Hilde is yours now, apparently,' Jonathan told him, gesturing to where the girl and Einar were deep in conversation.

'But I don't want a slave,' Max said.

'Not even Justine?' Jonathan said acidly.

Max shook his head. 'Not on Viking terms. What the hell am I going to do about Hilde?' He ran his hands through his blond hair. 'I know. I'll auction her off, and use the money to buy Justine off Svein.'

'I don't think you'd be allowed to do that,' Jonathan replied, 'and anyway, I think Svein would refuse to sell her. Look, why don't we sleep on the problem? We've still got Adrienne's ordeal to come, and once she's passed that, then we can decide what we're going to do about your surplus slave. Hey, maybe we could take her back to England with us.'

Max nodded, too weary to give the matter any serious consideration. He tried to imagine how the staff at Cavendish Publishing would react if he turned up at the office with a new secretary, one who spoke no English and who could be used to chase authors who missed their deadlines with a double-bladed axe. The thought kept him smiling all the way back to the village.

Chapter Eleven

Adrienne had the distinct feeling that she was living on borrowed time. She had watched the battle of endurance between Max and Hilde with a mixture of emotions. She had desperately wanted Max to win, but the way in which the men of the island had reacted to his victory had frightened and disturbed her. They saw no place in their society for a woman who did not conform to the desire to be a slave, and the way Hilde had capitulated to Max when he had beaten her in the wrestling match had only confirmed their arrogant belief that any woman could be brought to heel.

Adrienne did not subscribe to the notion that all women were naturally submissive, either mentally or sexually. True, she had very much enjoyed being spanked by Max, but that was merely a reversal of the role she usually played; if she did not have the facility to switch between dominance and submission, then the pleasure she took in sex would be greatly diminished. She knew from her exploits on campus back in Boston that for every latent submissive like Justine, there would be another who preferred to dominate, and half a dozen who had no desire to become involved in sadomasochistic games. She suspected that much the same was true of the women on Odinland, but they had gradually become accustomed to the notion that man was master and woman was slave, and it no longer occurred to them to change that pattern.

She would change it, if circumstances demanded it. Given the right man, she could persuade him that occasionally it was fun if the woman was on top – in every sense of the phrase. She simply had to find someone who was receptive to new thinking: someone like Erik. She shook her head sharply. Now, why was she thinking of him? Admittedly, he was their one real ally in the village, but that did not explain the mental picture she was painting of him, with the sun picking out the coppery highlights in his red-gold hair, and the way his woollen breeches had strained against his groin when he had been watching Svein punishing Justine. Lucky Justine, to have been taken by Erik in the forest. Adrienne tried to imagine how it would feel to have the length of his thick cock sliding into her tight anal hole while his big hands pawed at her heavy breasts...

'Adrienne?'

She started at the unexpected voice, looking up to see Gunvor standing before her. It had been decided that no one should be allowed to return to the little campsite on the far side of the island until all three ordeals had been completed, and so she had found herself sharing floor space with whoever had room for her. It was not an unpleasant arrangement. Tonight she was with Justine and Gunvor in Svein's hut, while Max and Jonathan slept with Einar and Erik. At least she had not been made to wear chains, and she was able to chat to Justine, who otherwise would not have heard a word of English all day, but she hated the atmosphere of fearful subservience the silversmith created around him. The little weasel was unworthy to call himself master, Adrienne thought. He ruled his charges with the hand of a bully, having none of the subtle erotic wiles at Max's disposal. When Max gave an order you wanted to obey it, because you knew the rewards would ultimately be sweet; you did what Svein told you simply because you were afraid he would hurt you.

Still, at least Svein was out with his cronies, playing dice games and drinking. He had instructed Gunvor to prepare some food for his return; the task completed, she had come to the back of the hut where Justine was dozing and Adrienne was trying her best not to think of whatever ordeal Einar might be inventing.

'Dinner's ready, then?' Adrienne said lightly.

'The pot's been set over the fire. I'll have to watch it; if I burn the food Svein always beats me,' Gunvor said, pushing loose strands of fair hair out of her eyes.

'Yeah, and if it isn't burnt, he'll still find some excuse to beat you,' Adrienne replied. 'Gunvor, how do you put up with the way he treats you?'

'I have no choice,' Gunvor replied simply. 'As long as I am owned by Svein, then I must do as he tells me.' She sighed. 'I envy Astrid. She was my fellow slave here until Svein gave her away, so that he might have Justine. She is in thrall to Snarri the weaver now. You might have seen him; he is blond, and he has a smooth face, like a boy. He is one of the most handsome men in the village. He is kinder than Svein and his punishments are meted out fairly. I think in time you might grow to love a man like that.'

Not me, sister, Adrienne thought. However good-looking and kind he was, I could never love a man just because he thought he owned me. She rose up on one elbow and looked at the Viking girl. 'Tell me, Gunvor, how did you become Svein's slave in the first place?'

'Well, I always knew I would be a slave to someone, as my mother must have been a slave to my father, though she died when I was born and I never knew her. My father died not long after, of a broken heart they said, and I lived with Einar's family, for Einar was my father's brother, and kinfolk look after each other here. I was brought up alongside Erik who is a couple of years older than me, and for a long time I thought that when we were both grown I might be given to him. I was always half in love with him, you see, and as the years passed my feelings for him grew stronger, though I could not put a name to them.

'By the time I had reached sixteen summers in age, Einar decided it was time I be given in thrall to the man who would master me. I know what you are thinking, Adrienne, but this is the way of our people, and I never thought to question it. If I had known that my lot was to become the slave of Svein the silversmith, I might have done as Hilde did, and tried to live a life free of all men, but I was still living with my dreams of lying beside Erik every night, as I always had done, but as his woman, rather than as his cousin.

'However, Einar decided I should be sold. I had long been told that I had a pretty face and a body to delight men, and he knew that the price he would get for me would keep him comfortably for a long time, for he was becoming an old man and work was harder for him. The night he told me this, I did not sleep at all. I went to Erik and begged him to lie with me, for I knew of what happens between a woman and a man, and I thought I would die if I could not experience it just once with him.

'He told me that my price would be lessened if I was not a virgin when I was sold, and that his father would kill him if he thought he had laid a hand on me. I spent the rest of the night lying awake, crying.

'When the morning came I was taken to the great hall. I was afraid, and all the more so when I saw the number of men who were there, waiting to bid for me. It was all over very quickly. I was stripped of my dress and the men were shown my naked body. They were making comments, and laughing, and saying what they would do to me when they owned me. Then they started bidding, and in only a few moments Svein was handing his money to Einar, and I was being taken away to his hut.

'He had another slave already, as I have said, and she was kind to me, for she had been bought and sold twice over, and she knew how lost and lonely I must be. Kind as she was she could not prepare me for the way Svein treated me. He made me sew up a tear in one of his tunics, and because I was nervous and unhappy, I pricked my finger with the bone needle and a little drop of my blood spilled onto the shirt. When Svein saw this he began ranting and raving and said I was a stupid, good-for-nothing girl who was not worth the money he had paid for me. He told me I had to learn what life was like in his hut; if I did something wrong I would have to be punished. Without any more ado, he grabbed hold of me and pulled my skirt up round my waist. I was wearing nothing beneath it and I knew both he and Astrid could see my bottom and my quim, and I blushed with the shame of it, as I had blushed when I had been paraded naked in the great hall before the men who wanted to buy me. Svein hauled me over his knee; you would not believe how strong he is, Adrienne, to say that he is so much smaller than the likes of Erik, but yet he was able to grip me and hold me in place with only one hand. I could not see what he was doing with the other, and then suddenly I felt a sharp blow on my backside, and I realised he had hit me with his palm, very hard. I had never been beaten by anyone until this moment, and I was not expecting anything like the pain I felt. I cried out, but he simply ignored me. His palm fell again, and again, and again, and each time it hurt like nothing I had known before. His hand moved all over my bottom, spanking and spanking, and then he began to hit me on the tops of my thighs, which hurt me even more. By now I was kicking my legs and squealing with the pain, and it did not occur to me that this meant my body was on show to him even more openly, because all I was trying to do was escape from that terrible pain. I wished I was back in Einar's hut, and I cried and called Erik every name under the sun for not having the bravery to stand up to his father and protect me from this, for I am sure that Einar knew what Svein was like, and yet he still took money from the man in payment for my services.

'And then something strange happened.' Gunvor's voice took on a new, softer tone. 'Although my bottom was smarting, and every slap that landed increased that smarting a little more, there was a different feeling, underneath the pain. I could not describe it, but it seemed like the same sensation I'd experienced when I put my hand between my legs and touched myself, thinking of Erik and the things I would like him to do to me. And that feeling was becoming stronger than the pain, taking my mind away from what was happening to me. And when Svein stopped spanking me and slid his hand underneath my body, touching me in the way I had touched myself, I felt my whole being shaking with powerful spasms, and my head was spinning and the blood was singing in my ears. I was still crying out, but now it was with pleasure.

'And then he threw me to the floor and took off his trousers. I could see his... his male thing, sticking up all hard and angry from his body. As I said, I knew of what happened when men and women lay together, and I knew that that great rod of flesh was supposed to fit into my body, but it seemed so big I could not see how.'

Adrienne, who had seen Svein's cock at the punishment post and knew it to be only average in size, smiled at Gunvor's naivety, and thought the girl should thank herself that Max Cavendish had not been the one who had taken her virginity. Though Max, she knew, would have been far more gentle and considerate than she supposed the silversmith to have been. Gunvor's next words bore her thoughts out.

'He parted my legs widely and lay over me, with that fleshy column of his between my thighs. And then he gave one big thrust, and pushed it right into me. I felt something tear within, and when I cried out this time, it was with sadness, for I knew he had taken something from me that I could never give again. He pumped his tool in and out of me until he was spent, and then he rolled off me and wiped himself on the hem of my dress.

'That was the first time he beat me, and the first time he lay with me, and nothing has ever changed since. He will still find the merest excuse to beat me, if he thinks I have done something wrong. Only the methods he uses to punish me have become more varied. Sometimes he hits me with his hand, sometimes with his belt, and sometimes with his whip. He likes to use the whip on my breasts, and sometimes he has even hit me between my legs. I always think he will whip me until I bleed, but he has never cut my skin. He knows I would not be able to work for a while if he did that, and I think that is what stops him, although he has told me that he loves the feel of my smooth white skin, and does not want to mark me permanently.' She shrugged. 'Perhaps he also knows that if he did, he would not get such a good price for me if he were to sell me again.

'The other thing that never changes is that when he punishes me, there is a part of me which enjoys it. My body always responds to him, and I am always ready for him to take me afterwards. But I still know that I would rather submit to a man who cares for me, who will punish me because I truly do deserve it and who will take his time in loving me afterwards.'

'There are men like that,' Adrienne said. 'Who knows, maybe one day Erik will have enough money to buy you from Svein.'

'I used to think that, too,' Gunvor said, her eyes filling with tears, 'but since Justine has come here I have seen the way he looks at her, and I think he would buy her if he had the chance.' She sniffed, miserably. 'I have seen the way he looks at you, too.'

'Oh, Gunvor,' Adrienne said, pulling the slave girl to her in an embrace. 'He looks at me the same way as the other men here do, because my skin is black and he's never seen anyone like me before. There's no more to it than that.'

Privately, she found herself hoping that he was looking at her with the thought that she would one day be his thrall. If she failed in her coming ordeal and condemned the others to a life of imprisonment on the island, Erik was the one man here to whom she would submit. Either that, or live free as Hilde had done. Having heard and seen how the likes of Svein treated their women, no other choice seemed bearable.

Justine wondered whether Adrienne and Gunvor were still talking. She glanced across, to see the two women in an embrace. For the hundredth time she wished that she could understand what was being said. When they ask me what I'd do if I could have my time over again, she thought, I'll tell them I'd take my Norse language option in the first year.

Still, she had things other than her non-existent grasp of the Norse tongue to worry about at the moment. Yesterday, she had found a long, thin sliver of metal on the floor when she had been clearing up after Svein. He had not noticed it, or if he had, he had obviously thought it was of no use, but to Justine it was a way out of this miserable place. She had tucked it into the bodice of her dress, waiting for a time when Svein left her alone in the hut. When he had announced that he was off to gamble with his friends, she had almost cheered. Gunvor had told her that on these occasions he normally stayed out half the night, and that would give her ample time to do what she needed. She took the metal sliver out of her dress and inserted it into the lock in her ankle cuffs, rotating it experimentally. When she had seen a similar technique used in films, it seemed to take only seconds before the lock was springing open. In real life things were not so easy. She jiggled the metal, careful to make as little noise as she could, but nothing seemed to be happening. For long minutes she probed and experimented, until she began to believe that lock picking was a non-existent skill, invented by the authors of Victorian detective novels. And then there was a tiny, barely audible click. She tugged at the cuff, which suddenly felt looser around her ankle, and felt it come away. She hardly dared believe it was happening, but she had freed herself.

Again she looked over to Adrienne and Gunvor. Their embrace appeared to be more intimate now; Adrienne's hands had disappeared into the folds of the other girl's dress, while her own skirt appeared to be rucked up around her thighs, revealing glimpses of her firm, dark-skinned bottom. The young Viking slave was uttering gentle sighs and gasps of pleasure. Neither of them would notice if she went missing. Justine felt a brief stab of guilt; she should be trying to free everyone, not just herself. But if she could find Jonathan and Max, they could come back and rescue Adrienne.

Without another backward glance, she quietly began to creep out of Svein's home. She emerged from the dim, smoky atmosphere of the hut, trying to accustom her eyes to the starlit darkness outside. She had gone about half a yard, scurrying on her hands and knees, when she put her palm down on something hard and leathery. Something that felt suspiciously like a boot. She glanced up, sensing rather than seeing a dark shape in front of her, and felt a sudden sick fear in the pit of her stomach.

The shape spoke. She could not understand the words, but she recognised instantly the low, sinister voice. It was Svein; back early from his evening's pleasure. Back far too early for Justine's liking.

He reached down and grabbed her hair, tugging on the roots till she cried out. Her reaction was not fuelled by pain alone; she wanted to alert Adrienne and Gunvor to the fact that something was wrong. She wanted to prevent Svein bursting in and catching them as they made love to each other. She did not know how he felt about his slaves taking their erotic pleasure in his absence, but she assumed he would not be happy. Nothing anyone did which was not the result of one of his express orders seemed to make him happy.

However, going into the hut appeared to be the last thing on Svein's mind. He dragged Justine to her feet and began to haul her out of the village. She knew exactly where he was taking her; she still bore some of the bruises from her last encounter with the punishment post, and she had been hoping it would be a long time before she found herself in that cursed circle of stones once more. Her hopes were about to be dashed.

She looked around vainly for someone who might notice where she was being taken, but they seemed to be entirely alone in the darkness. Perhaps Svein's money had run out earlier than he had planned, and he had either decided to call it a night, or come back for further supplies. Whatever, the general fun and games appeared not to have broken up. No one would know where she was. No one would miss her.

Svein was walking so fast she could barely keep up with him. She tried to hang back, forcing him to slow his pace, but the silversmith would not be distracted from his purpose. If he had had a bad night playing cards, or the board game with the incomprehensible rules they called *hnefatafl*, then he would be looking for a scapegoat on which he could take out his displeasure.

It did not take them long to reach the punishment post. Justine looked up fearfully at the lengths of chain that dangled from the shadowy post. She could not stop remembering how it had felt to hang from those chains, her body spinning out of control under the force of Svein's blows, never knowing when or where the next was going to land. He could not put her through such an ordeal again. She was quickly realising her tolerance for punishment, and Svein always seemed determined to exceed that tolerance. With no witnesses around to control his excesses, she was afraid he might seriously hurt her.

Fortunately he did not seem to want to chain her to the post. It seemed that he simply wanted the protection that carrying out a punishment within the circle of stones offered him. Instead, he ordered her down onto her elbows and knees, forcing her body into the required position with the aid of the odd kick at her backside. Eventually she crouched in place, her face almost flat against the hard earth, her bottom raised high in the air, her knees about a foot apart. It was a position designed to display her intimate parts and maximise her humiliation. Her discomfort was increased when Svein grabbed the hem of her dress and pulled it up to her shoulders, baring her smooth, pale back and buttocks to his gaze.

She heard a noise behind her, realised it was Svein unbuckling his belt, and knew instantly what her punishment would consist of. She tried to prepare herself for the feel of the thick, supple leather landing hard against her flesh, knowing that even Svein was not such a sadist that he would hit her with the buckle end. Or perhaps he would only refrain because he did not want to damage something he had created himself.

All further thought was driven from her mind as the belt whistled through the air and landed with a crack on her buttocks. She gasped as a bolt of pain shot through her, knowing that this was only the first of many and wanting to dig herself deep into the dirt to avoid them.

Again the belt landed, parallel to the first. Svein was intending to stripe her arse thoroughly. A third came, this one lower, catching the softest and most fleshy part of her cheeks, and she howled. She sought to ride the waves of agony that pulsed through her, praying for him to stop as another swipe of the belt caught her on the back. He was catching bruises that were only just fading from her last punishment, reawakening old wounds.

She knew that part of her needed the pain to stimulate areas of her sexuality she had never known existed until Max had first alerted her to them, but when Svein punished her it was only for his own gratification. Even if Justine had been able to articulate her needs, Svein would simply have ignored them. His enjoyment and his orgasm were all that mattered.

The fire she felt in her nerve-endings flared up again as Svein continued to beat her with his belt. The heavy leather was raising thick weals on her skin, and Svein paused to run his fingers over them. Tears were streaming from Justine's eyes, and she would have begged him to stop if she had not known that the sight of her, reduced to incoherent pleading, would simply have aroused him all the more.

If Max had been beating her she knew she would have been begging, but it would have been to feel his cock sliding into her sex, and his skilful fingers pinching her nipples into hard, aching peaks. But what she really wanted, she realised as Svein's belt landed sharply against the tender backs of her thighs, was to be on the receiving end of a punishment from Jonathan. When he had come to her on the last night of his ordeal – and she was sure it had been him, whatever common sense might have told her that he was locked in a wooden cage somewhere in the forest – he had showed a side of his character she had never seen before. He had acted then as though he knew what it meant to dominate a woman, and she had welcomed the new, cruel and demanding Jonathan with willingness. He should be her master, not this selfish,

179

sadistic Viking.

In her mind it became Jonathan who was wielding the belt, and somehow that seemed to make the pain more bearable. At last, she heard Svein toss the belt to the ground and felt his fingers probing between her legs. She was wet, turned on by her mental images of Jonathan, and Svein's inquiring digits moved smoothly over her slick labia. The silversmith grunted, and the next thing she knew it was the head of his cock that was pressing against her sex lips. With an involuntary motion she widened her legs slightly further, feeling his glans nudging at the tight ring of muscle at the entrance to her vagina. He pushed hard, lodging himself snugly inside her, and began to thrust. He was still wearing his woollen breeches and his shirt, and she felt the coarse material scratching against the weals he had raised on her bottom and thighs.

If Svein's previous performances were anything to go by, he would be so turned on by having chastised her that he would not last long, certainly not long enough for her to reach her own orgasm. She wanted to reach down and touch her own clitoris, to give herself the stimulation she craved, but with her head down and her elbows flat against the ground, as Svein had ordered, that was impossible. Instead, she closed her eyes and pictured Jonathan thrusting into her, imagined the feel of his hands on her breasts and the subtle, masculine smell of him. Combined with the fast, erratic rhythm of Svein's member rubbing against the inner walls of her sex, it was enough to bring her to the point of climax.

Just before he came, Svein pulled out, spending his seed over the cheeks of her backside. The feel of the viscous liquid beginning to cool on her skin was the last thing she registered before her orgasm hit her.

Svein was noticeably more cheerful as he urged her to her feet and began to lead her back to the village. Justine thought of Adrienne, and the final ordeal that was to come the following day. Whatever happened then would determine whether or not they spent the rest of their lives on this island. Max and Jonathan had ridden their luck outrageously, and Adrienne had to do the same. The prospect if she failed was almost too hideous to contemplate.

Chapter Twelve

Max had never thought he would miss the tedious physical work of Jonathan's dig, but he would have given anything to have a spade in his hand and a mindless, repetitive task to perform. He neglected to remind himself that he had spent only part of a morning fetching and carrying while Jonathan and Adrienne marked out the site; now that he had nothing to do but wait for Einar to set the last of their three ordeals, he was looking back on his brief spell as a would-be archaeologist with rose tinted enthusiasm.

He would have been happy to go back to the little campsite and hunt out the short-wave radio that had been part of their equipment. Anything which reminded them there was a larger world outside this weird island would have been most welcome. Einar had taken his wristwatch away 'for safe keeping' when he had stripped naked to fight Hilde, and he doubted whether it would be given back to him. His body clock was adjusting to Odinland time and the natural rhythms of dawn and dusk, but he craved a return to the world he had known before.

If Jonathan was bored, too – and Max suspected that a man of his enquiring intellect would be – he did not show it. He was still obsessed with Justine's safety.

Adrienne had told him that his girlfriend had been taken out by Svein and given a thorough beating in the middle of the night, apparently for trying to escape, though she had been vague on the details, claiming she had been otherwise occupied at the time. If left alone with Svein, Max knew that Jonathan would kill him, and he had to admit that if his brother asked, he would help him in the task.

He yawned and scratched himself. He would give anything for a long, hot soak in the tub and a change of clothes. Max thought sadly of the Armani suits and crisp white Gieves and Hawkes shirts hanging in his wardrobe in his home back in Suffolk, and wondered if he would ever wear any of them again. Even the spare pair of worn jeans and the red and white rugby shirt that was packed away in his rucksack would have felt like heaven next to his skin, though that part of the island was still strictly off-limits to him.

Perhaps something could be arranged. Hilde was sitting by the fire, plucking a chicken. Although she was beginning to settle into the life of a slave – his slave, for better or worse – and was losing some of her wild ways, the vigour with which she wrenched the feathers from the dead bird sent an uneasy shiver down Max's spine.

He caught the girl's eye and beckoned her over. She wiped her fingers on her dress as she came. There was a wooden tub that Einar and Erik used for bathing hanging from a hook on the wall, and he gestured to her to lift it down. He could have done the job easily himself, but Hilde had to learn her place.

He lifted the empty pot that was used for boiling water, and mimed filling it from the stream. Hilde watched him for a moment, puzzled, then realised what he was asking of her. She nodded her head, took the pot from him, and went outside, returning moments later having filled it to the brim. In her absence he had stoked the fire, and he watched with approval as she set the heavy pot over the smouldering embers.

It took three pots of hot water to fill the tub to an acceptable level. When Max was finally happy, he shrugged off his clothes, and stepped into the water. He was aware of Hilde's eyes on his naked body, her gaze fixed somewhere around his cock, as he settled down and made himself comfortable in the small tub. Hilde was holding the soap; it was a grubby grey mixture of animal fat and ashes, and he eyed it with mild distaste. He would have preferred a bar of Imperial Leather and a bottle of decent shampoo, but knew he would have to make do with what he was given. He reached for the soap, but Hilde shook her head. She dipped her hand into the water, lathering up the soap as best she could, and rubbed it on Max's back.

This he could get used to, he thought, closing his eyes. She was thorough in her attentions, massaging his shoulder muscles and the length of his spine. He began to relax as she rinsed the soap away and turned her attention to his chest, more than happy to let her lavish her attention on him in this way.

Eventually, her hands strayed below the waterline, seeking his cock where it slumbered against his thigh. His eyes snapped open abruptly and he caught hold of her wrist as he felt her fingers wrap themselves around his shaft. 'Did I give you permission to touch me there?' he asked.

In his relaxed state he had forgotten she could not understand, but when he pulled her hand out of the water and glared at it, she blushed and dropped her head. She looked so delicious in that moment that Max could not resist yanking her in the direction of the tub. Despite her strength, she was caught off-balance, and toppled into the water on top of him. Enraged, she struggled and fought like the warrior she had been until so recently, but Max held her fast, knowing he had the mental superiority in this battle. Her dress was soaked, the thin woollen material clinging to the contours of her breasts and hips, and she did not object when he stripped it from her and threw it to the ground.

Despite her annoyance, she was laughing now, her wet body slippery as an eel in his grasp. There was no real room for them to manoeuvre in the tub, but Max could feel Hilde reaching for his cock again.

'Slow down, woman. All in good time,' he muttered good-humouredly. He was already almost fully erect, and the feel of her greedy fingers hardened him further. In this position, with her body half on top of his, her buttocks were presented enticingly, droplets of water glistening on her honey-gold skin. Unable to turn down such blatant provocation, Max brought his hand down sharply on her backside, feeling the strange sensation of her wet flesh beneath his palm. She yelped and wriggled, which only encouraged him to do it again.

A light of devilment in her eyes, Hilde rose up briefly and plunged down on to Max's shaft, taking his whole length inside her body. He laughed, feeling her tight muscles clenching around him, and renewed his assault on her buttocks. Each slap caused her to bob up and down on his cock, and he realised it would not take much of this to make him come. He sighed, torn between the desire to prolong the fuck and the urge to tan Hilde's wanton backside. The latter consideration won out, and he spanked her hard, loving the way she squealed and protested. Her movements were becoming more urgent, now, her velvet sheath clasping him as though she could never bear to let him go. Her fingers reached down and began to rub her clitoris, her expression almost beatific as she approached orgasm.

Max clasped her taut arse cheeks, urging her harder down onto his prick, feeling his own climax rushing unstoppably through his body. His cock spasmed and released its creamy load deep in Hilde's tight channel, and she cried out something which sounded suspiciously like his own name as she came.

'Max! Max!' This time it was Jonathan calling his name, he realised, as his brother burst into the hut.

'Is something wrong?' Max asked, his voice languid with the aftermath of good sex.

'No, just get dressed and make yourself look halfway decent,' Jonathan replied. 'Einar will be back any second. It's time for Adrienne to find out what her ordeal is going to be.'

Max urged Hilde to stand up, and he got out of the rapidly cooling water. Soft, fluffy towels were yet another luxury item unknown to the Vikings, he realised as Hilde handed him a thin piece of cloth to dry himself with. Whatever the task Adrienne was about to receive, she had to pass it, if only so that he could return to a land that appreciated its creature comforts.

'These are the teeth of Fafnir,' Einar announced, handing two small pieces of metal to Adrienne. She weighed them in her hand, recognising their approximate shape and function. 'If you can bear their bite for the specified time, you will have passed the final ordeal.'

'What on earth are they?' Jonathan asked, taking them from her and studying them curiously.

'Nipple clamps, unless I'm much mistaken,' Max told

him. 'It seems our hosts are even more advanced in the art of punishment than I took them to be.'

'So Adrienne is going to have these – these things attached to her nipples?' Jonathan was aghast. 'That's barbaric.'

Max shook his head. 'You have got a lot to learn, brother.' He turned to Adrienne. 'Have you ever used these before?'

'Used, yes. Worn, no.' She looked at them again, trying to imagine what it would feel like to have the little metal vices fastened to her sensitive nipples. 'There's a first time for everything, though, I suppose. And after all, submissives get to experience these all the time, and they seem to cope okay. How difficult can it be?'

She was regretting the lightness of her tone. The clamps had been in place for over three hours now, and she had lost all feeling in her nipples. Things had not been helped by the manner in which they had been affixed. The whole event had taken on an air of ritual. A young pine tree had been chopped down and stripped of its branches. The trunk had been buried in the earth, in the centre of the village. As Adrienne had watched this taking place she had realised that her ordeal, like Max's, was to take on a very public aspect.

Once the wooden post was securely in place, Einar and Snarri the weaver between them had taken Adrienne to stand by it, each holding her arms securely, so she could not escape from them. She had wondered why this was necessary, considering that she was undergoing this ordeal voluntarily, but had soon realised they were trying to enforce their superiority over her.

She had been made to stand with her back against the tree trunk, her arms behind her and crossed at the wrists.

A few turns of thick rope had served first to bind her hands together, and then to tie her to the post. This done, the blond-haired, handsome Snarri had taken hold of the front of Adrienne's top and torn it roughly in two. She wore no bra beneath it, and those who were standing around watching had given an appreciative murmur at the sight of her heavy, unfettered breasts, with their large, aubergine-coloured nipples.

Now Einar had stepped forward, clutching the two metal clamps. He had taken hold of Adrienne's left breast, holding it more tightly and for far longer than was strictly necessary to attach the clamp. She had bitten her lip as he twisted the clamp into place, feeling the metal pinch at her tender nipple, but did her best to show no other outward emotion. That done, he had fastened its twin to her right nipple, and stood back to admire his handiwork. A strange smile had played around his lips.

'I forgot to mention,' he had said, 'that while you are wearing the teeth of Fafnir, those around you have the right to touch or play with whatever part of your body they see fit, just as the dragon for whom they are named would play with his prey before he despatched it. If at any time you feel that the bite of the teeth is too much for you to bear, then you must simply say, but you have only to keep them in place until sundown to ensure the freedom of your friend, Justine. It is not too much to ask, now is it?'

That's easy for you to say, Adrienne had thought. It was early afternoon, which meant she would have to keep these wretched clamps in place for the best part of five or six hours. They had not been too painful at that moment, but as they deadened the flow of blood to her nipples they would really begin to make their presence felt. And when they were removed… 'I'll be fine,' she had replied defiantly.

Einar had gone back to his hut, laughing to himself, and most of the onlookers had drifted back to their chores, but Snarri the weaver had stayed behind. He obviously wanted to take advantage of the freedom he had been given to touch and fondle Adrienne's body, for his fine-boned hands had reached out to grasp at her generous breasts. Adrienne had borne the onslaught as he had stroked her puckering areolae, trying not to acknowledge the fact that his subtle touch was sending little arrows of excitement down from her nipples to her womb.

She had wondered what he was going to do to her next, for he was clearly enjoying having her at his mercy, but he had been called away by one of the other men to help in the rounding-up of a couple of stray goats, leaving her alone only with the greatest of reluctance.

However, he had only been the first of a procession of curious men who had wanted to touch and enjoy the body of this strange, dark-skinned beauty who was unlike any other woman they had ever seen. Hands had fondled her breasts, and cupped her firm buttocks through the long, loose skirt she wore. The villagers had a tendency to approach her from behind, so that she did not always know whose fingers were arousing her nerve-endings to a peak of erotic sensation. She had never known quite how stimulating an anonymous caress could be, until now.

Eventually, they had become bolder, one taking hold of her clothing where Snarri had already torn it, and pulling it away completely from the upper half of her body. Fingers had flicked the nipple clamps she wore, sending a sudden jolt of pain through the numb buds. And then, inevitably, her skirt had been torn away from her, leaving her in

189

nothing but a strangely virginal pair of white cotton panties, from which tufts of her luxuriant black pubic hair escaped.

She had been even more vulnerable in her almost naked state, passers-by taking the opportunity to rub her vulva through the thin cotton. She had not wanted to succumb to their touch, but, traitorously, her legs had moved apart of their own accord, inviting anyone who wanted to fondle her between them. It had been Thorulf, the pudgy-faced man who had been the third party in the bidding war for Justine, who had finally grasped the waistband of Adrienne's panties and tugged them down to her knees. His fingers had immediately delved into her bush of dark curls, seeking the slightly parted lips and protruding clitoris beneath them. He had rubbed rapidly at her moist sex flesh, stimulating her in a way that was guaranteed to bring her to a swift orgasm. Just as she was teetering on the brink of a climax, he had withdrawn his fingers. She had begged with him to continue, but he had simply laughed and gone on his way.

From the position of the sun in the sky, Adrienne reckoned that had happened almost an hour ago. Since then she had been subject to regular visits from Snarri, Thorulf and a couple of the other village men. They had run their hands over her breasts and bottom, or insinuated a couple of fingers into her juicy cleft, probing her vagina and her anal hole. They had casually and contemptuously flicked or tugged the clamps that were so firmly attached to her nipples, sending a spasm of pain through her body that somehow mingled with the pleasure she felt at their caresses. Every time, these caresses had stopped at just the moment when Adrienne's body was limp and trembling in her bonds, her skin streaked with sweat and her throat bared, on the verge of orgasm. This prolonged sexual

190

stimulation, which always halted just short of resolution, had left her utterly frustrated. She had no way of bringing herself to climax, and though she pleaded with them to let her come, they stubbornly refused. She knew this was all part of her humiliation, but she could not prevent her body from responding.

She heard footsteps behind her, and tensed in readiness for another onslaught on her erogenous zones. It did not come. Instead, her latest visitor walked round to stand in front of her, looking at her with a mixture of arousal and concern. It was Erik.

Adrienne felt a sudden pulse beating strongly between her legs as he feasted his eyes on her naked, glistening body. He had never seen her naked before, and she experienced a moment of unexpected coyness, wishing to shield her breasts and pubic triangle from his gaze.

'Did your dad send you to gloat?' Adrienne asked. 'Do the two of you get off on the thought of me here, being pawed by whoever feels like it?'

'You are doing well, Adrienne,' Erik replied, ignoring the venom in her voice. 'Almost any other woman would have been begging to have the clamps removed by now. Like your friends, you have uncommon courage.'

'So don't you want to join in the fun? Take advantage of my body like everyone else has?' As she spoke the words, she found herself willing his hands to reach out and cup her breasts; for him to go further than any of the others had, and thrust his cock into her.

'I would like nothing more, but I have another purpose in being here,' Erik told her.

Adrienne realised he was holding something in his hands. 'What's that?' she asked.

He held it up. It was a length of heavy silver chain,

about nine inches in length. Svein's handiwork, Adrienne supposed. She had to acknowledge that the man was a fine craftsman, whatever his personality defects. Thinking about him prevented her from dwelling too long on the implications of the chain itself.

'As you are more than halfway through the ordeal, my father feels it is time that the severity of the test is increased. I have been told to attach each end of this chain to the clamps. You know how it will feel as the weight of the chain pulls on them, don't you?' His fingers were toying with the clamp on her right nipple as he spoke, sending a sharp twinge of erotic pain through the sensitive tissue. She bit her lip, feeling her juices flowing more strongly in response to his touch.

'I would like to see this hanging between those beautiful breasts of yours permanently, Adrienne.' Erik said, as he fastened the chain in place. 'I have heard it is how the Nubian women adorn themselves. If you were mine I would pierce your nipples, and you would wear a ring in each one as a token of your servitude.'

'If I was yours, I would wear them gladly,' Adrienne replied quietly, almost unable to believe what she was saying. She had always believed her role was to be the dominant one, but now she wanted nothing more than to give herself over utterly to this man's will. This was nothing like the sudden need she had felt to switch to when in Max's company. With Erik, she would be making the conscious gesture to become his slave, and the thought frightened and exhilarated her.

Erik tugged at the chain, to check it was secure, and she almost screamed aloud.

'Poor, tortured nipples,' Erik murmured, running a gentle finger over the swollen flesh. 'I hope I shall be the one who is allowed to release them from the dragon's teeth.'

Adrienne tried not to think how it would feel when the blood finally flooded back into the tender buds. 'You said you wanted to take advantage of my body,' she whispered. 'Do it, please.'

Erik needed no second bidding. His hands were on her breasts in a heartbeat, lifting and pressing them together. The silver chain sparkled in the sunlight, contrasting with the blackness of Adrienne's skin, and for a moment she could imagine how it would feel to have her nipples linked by that chain as a visible symbol of her submission.

His mouth was on her throat in a kiss that became a bite, his small, sharp teeth nipping her skin and bruising it, marking her as his own. Adrienne moaned, feeling his hands move lower, down over the flatness of her stomach and round to clasp her buttocks. Now he was biting her breasts, so inflamed by passion that he was like a wild animal. She wished her hands were free, so that she could pull at his long, red-gold hair, and scrape her nails the length of his back. He roused in her the primitive need to claw and scratch, to leave visible marks of her desire on his skin.

Instead, she could only urge him on with words of lust, begging him to treat her as roughly as he wished. He smiled, and the soft, stroking motions of his hands on her buttocks suddenly became a forceful slap. She shuddered. 'That's what I need, Erik,' she moaned. 'Spank me hard.'

He moved round so that he was standing behind her, the better to do as she wished. His palm came down on the parts of her backside that were not pressed against the post she was tied to, again and again. The power of his blows caused her to writhe in her bonds, the length of chain between her breasts jiggling and pulling on the nipple clamps, but she no longer cared about the discomfort those clamps were inflicting, or about the dull ache in her arse cheeks. She had crossed the threshold between agony and ecstasy, and was moving closer to her long-denied orgasm.

His hand caught the crease of her buttock, where it joined her thigh, and she yelped, maddened and unbearably turned on. She would do anything, if only he would carry on inflicting that bittersweet pain. Suddenly, Erik stopped what he was doing. Adrienne could have cried out in her frustration. Like every other man, he seemed determined to take her to the edge and leave her dangling. And she had been foolish enough to think he was different. Did he want her to beg and abase herself? Was he only interested in completing the humiliation the likes of Snarri and Thorulf had begun? Or did he want her to acquiesce to the removal of the nipple clamps, her orgasm guaranteed if she gave up her attempts to succeed with her ordeal?

His next action made her wonder why she had doubted him. He came to stand before her once more, and let his breeches drop to his knees. Adrienne gasped at the length and thickness of his member, which rose proud and erect from the red nest of hair at the apex of his thighs. His fingers sought between her legs, parting her inner lips, and he pressed the head of his cock to the entrance of her sex. She mewled her acceptance, almost crazed with the need to feel him inside her.

The blunt cockhead lodged itself within her juicy channel, and then he thrust his hips once, filling her to the hilt. His body was pressed against hers, the hated nipple clamps digging into his chest as he took her. His thrusts were fierce and powerful, and she cried out as she felt him stabbing against the neck of her womb. The blood was pounding in her ears and she fought for breath as her orgasm hit her. For a moment she almost lost consciousness, and then Erik was coming too, the jerking motions of his cock wrenching a second, unexpected climax from her.

He pulled out of her and stood for a moment, looking at her as she hung in her bonds, recovering. His expression was utterly wretched.

'Erik, what's wrong?' she asked softly.

'I should not have done that,' he replied, 'and yet I knew I could not live if I did not have you, just once. I know how strong you are, Adrienne. I know you will pass the ordeal, and then you will be gone from me.'

'But you know why I have to pass,' Adrienne said.

Erik nodded. 'And I want you to. I want Justine to go free, and I want to see you all return safely to the world you came from. No, that is a lie. I would be happy to see Justine return, and Jonathan and Max, but I yearn to keep you here, to make you my slave.'

'Erik, don't say that,' Adrienne said. 'You know that isn't going to happen.'

'I know.' He sighed. 'All too soon, Einar will come here. He will see that you still wear the teeth of Fafnir, and that nothing that's been done to you has broken your spirit. And then it will all be over.'

'I hope so,' Adrienne said, wishing she could tell him how she felt about him without jeopardising the safety of her friends. 'I really hope so.'

Chapter Thirteen

Max woke with a sour taste in his mouth and the sensation that someone was dancing a flamenco in the back of his skull. The night before was a blur of jumbled images that had begun at sunset when he and Jonathan had been taken by Erik to watch Einar release Adrienne from her bondage. He recalled the way she had reacted to the removal of the nipple clamps with a cry of pure anguish, and how she had leaned against Erik as the big Viking had slowly and very gently massaged the life back into her breasts. If Max remembered rightly, Erik had gone on massaging them long after the point when she would have no longer felt any pain, and she had not seemed to object.

They had been taken to the great hall, where the slaves had been preparing a feast in readiness. Max suppressed the thought that if Adrienne had not been successful in her ordeal, that meal would have been eaten to celebrate her own induction into slavery and his and Jonathan's uncertain fate. Jonathan had wanted Justine to be handed over by Svein then and there, but Einar had told him that could wait until the morning. Instead, she had spent the evening sitting on the floor between Jonathan and Svein, while the two men vied to feed her with the choicest titbits of meat from their own plates. There had been a ritual performance given by Thorulf and his slave girl, Astrid, while the meal had taken place. She had been bound to a wooden frame, and Thorulf had used an intricately plaited whip to stripe the length of the redhead's pale, freckled back and buttocks, to the hearty approval of all the men watching. Max remembered little of this event, due to the fact that he had been constantly plied with mead, the sharp, sweetish drink tasting innocuous but having a stronger kick than any of the home-made ciders he was used to purchasing from the farms close to where he lived.

He had slept late, and the sun was high in the sky. Beside him, there was the hollow imprint of Jonathan's body on the straw, but his brother was nowhere to be seen. Max brushed a hand through his hair and straightened his crumpled clothes. He could not shake the feeling that today was significant for some reason other than the end of the trials the four of them had gone through.

Erik was sitting outside the hut, whittling a piece of wood with his knife. Adrienne was by his side. She looked up as Max approached. 'Have you seen Jonathan?' he asked.

'He went over to see Svein about ten minutes ago,' Adrienne replied. 'He's gone to get Justine back. I thought they'd have it sorted by now, to tell the truth.'

There was a sudden, angry shout from the direction of Svein's hut.

'That doesn't sound too promising,' Max said. 'I'm off to find out what's going on.'

Svein and Jonathan were standing outside the silversmith's hut, squaring up to each other. If the hatred had not been etched so vividly on Svein's face, Jonathan would have smiled at the sight of the smaller man growling at him like a bad-tempered terrier. It was the only thing about the situation that was amusing. He had come here expecting to take Justine away from her hated would-be master, but Svein was refusing to agree to the terms of the deal they had agreed with Einar.

'You can't have her,' Svein was repeating.

'But she's mine,' Jonathan replied. 'Last night we feasted together as – well, friends would be stretching it a bit – and now you're supposed to hand her over.'

'Supposed to, perhaps,' Svein said, playing up to his newly-arrived audience. 'Like you were supposed to lose those ordeals, and you passed them all with the help of your strangers' magic.'

'Magic? What magic?' Jonathan looked baffled.

'There must have been some sorcery involved,' Svein asserted. 'How else could you have survived three days in the cage of Syn? How else could your brother have defeated the woman no one else could tame? And how else could your Nubian slave have resisted the bite of Fafnir's teeth? You brought strange pieces of trickery with you, like those metal sundials you wore on your wrists.'

'Yes, the same sundials which have been locked in this chest,' Adrienne said, producing the box in which Einar had placed all their valuables. 'And the chest has been locked – until now.'

Erik handed her the key and she unlocked the box, distributing the watches and other personal possessions it contained to their rightful owners.

Max gave an anguished shout as he strapped his watch back on to his wrist. Jonathan broke off from arguing with Svein and stared at him.

'Max, what's wrong?' he asked.

'Look at the date,' Max replied, pointing to the display on the watch face. 'I should have realised. This is the day your friend Bud comes to take us back to the airport at

Newfoundland. If he's running to schedule, he'll be here in less than half an hour.'

'Then we can't mess about any longer.' Jonathan pushed Svein out of the way and ran inside the hut. 'Gunvor, where's the key to Justine's chains?' he asked.

'In the little wooden box on the topmost shelf,' Gunvor replied. 'What are you doing? You can't unfasten those chains without Svein's permission.'

'Oh, yes, I can,' Jonathan replied. 'And don't worry, if Svein lays a finger on you for giving me that information, I'll make sure Erik beats him within an inch of life. It's about time he got a taste of his own medicine.'

As Jonathan spoke, he was unlocking the chains that kept Justine prisoner. She rose to her feet, unsteady after a long night in bondage, and Jonathan hugged her tightly to him, kissing her full on the lips.

Outside, he could hear shouting, some of it in guttural Norse, the rest in Max's calm Home Counties inflexions. He and Justine dashed out to see Svein's hands reaching to grasp Max's throat, while Erik did his best to separate the two.

As Einar pulled Svein away, Max lashed out with his fist, catching the silversmith squarely on his nose. There was a faint crack, and blood spurted from Svein's nostrils. Jonathan was torn between applauding and running, but his instinct for self-preservation won out.

'Come on, let's go,' he shouted. 'Max, take the girls and head for the beach. I'll go to the campsite and salvage as much of the stuff as I can.'

'I shall come with you,' Erik told him. 'An extra pair of hands will be useful for you, and I fear you may need some protection.' He gestured to where Svein had accosted a couple of the village men. The silversmith was gesticulating wildly, pointing to his ruined nose, and then to Jonathan. One of the men snatched up a heavy hammer that was lying on the ground. That was Jonathan's cue to flee the village. He took one last backward glance to make sure that Max, Justine and Adrienne were on their way to the rendezvous point, and then he and Erik were running for their lives.

Max's heart was hammering in his chest as he rounded the crest of a hill and found himself looking down on the long, deserted stretch of beach. Above him, he heard a distant buzzing noise, and looked up to see a small dot in the sky that grew larger as it descended. Bud's plane, the most welcome sight in the world.

Adrienne and Justine ran down to the firm grey sand and began to wave, attracting the pilot's attention. Max followed them, his feet skidding on the loose shingle of the makeshift cliff path. He looked round, expecting to see Svein and the other village men. It had taken the silversmith a few minutes to mobilise his allies to follow him, and that had given Max and the girls a comfortable head start, but they could not be far behind, now. Unless they had gone after Jonathan and Erik. It seemed unlikely, given that Max was the one who had broken Svein's nose, but the man's mind worked in a strange and sadistic way, and he might want to have the satisfaction of despatching Jonathan, just so he could have the pleasure of breaking the news of his death to Justine. Grisly images of the silversmith holding Jonathan's severed head aloft in triumph danced in Max's mind, and he forced himself to get a grip on reality.

And then Jonathan's head was appearing over the edge of the cliff, Erik's red-gold one beside it. Max waved and pointed to the plane. Jonathan nodded and began his slow descent, hampered by the weight of the rucksacks he was carrying. Erik had some of their precious equipment in his hands, but Max knew that the tents themselves had been left behind, and he could not see the short-wave radio among their possessions.

The plane's wheels were down and it was coming in to land. It rolled along the sand, gradually losing speed, and came to rest close to the shore. Justine was doing her best to wrench open the door, not even waiting for the engine to come to a halt, and Max realised the reason for her urgency. A dozen men were on the cliff path, brandishing swords and axes, and heading rapidly in their direction.

As quickly as they could, Max, Jonathan and Erik loaded up the plane with everything that had been rescued from the campsite.

'They followed us all the way,' Jonathan explained, fighting to catch his breath as he worked. 'I thought we were dead. They want our blood. Not Erik's, but mine and yours, Max. They're demanding a sacrifice to Thor.'

'Well, they can keep on demanding it,' Max retorted. 'If that's the last of the rucksacks we can get in the plane and go.'

Justine was already on board and Jonathan quickly joined her. Max waited for Adrienne to climb inside, but she and Erik were in each other's arms, talking in low voices.

'Adrienne, get in the plane!' Max ordered.

'I'm sorry, Max, I'm not coming with you,' Adrienne replied.

Max stared at her in disbelief. 'What the hell are you talking about?'

'I want to stay here.' Adrienne stared levelly back at him. 'I love Erik, and I want to be with him. I want to be his slave.'

'So much for the dominant Dr Devaney,' Max quipped, remembering how eagerly Adrienne had submitted to him in that New York hotel room. It seemed like half a lifetime ago. He took what he supposed would be his last look at her, her dark hair being whipped across her face by the breeze, and realised that there were tears in her eyes. Erik's brawny arm was flung protectively round her shoulders, and Max knew that if she was entering into voluntary slavery at the hands of this big Viking, she would be safe, stranger to this island or not. She was willing to become part of this alien society, and Max knew that if she had any regrets, she was burying them deeply. From what he knew of her home and work life, he doubted that was the case: there were few who were close enough to Adrienne to miss her, though he wondered what story he and Jonathan would tell on their return to America when asked to explain why the beautiful academic was no longer with them.

If they returned to America, that was. Svein and the other villagers were only a few hundred yards from the plane now, and advancing swiftly. The rays of the early-morning sun glinted on the weapons they carried; weapons their ancestors had bequeathed them when they gave up the need to fight so many generations ago. Max clasped Erik and Adrienne in one last embrace.

'Don't worry about me, I'll be fine,' Adrienne assured him. 'I'll have Hilde to keep me company. We might even manage to teach the women here that they can be on top for a change.'

Max smiled. 'Well, if anyone can, you can.'

'Good luck, Max,' Adrienne whispered. 'Tell Jon and Justine goodbye from me.'

Erik clutched at Max's arm and nodded. No words passed between them, since for all their efforts they still could not understand each other, but his meaning was clear. Max nodded back and disappeared into the little plane, pulling the door shut tightly behind him.

The light craft began to trundle along the beach, Bud attempting to pick up enough speed to achieve take-off. The Vikings were almost keeping up with the plane; Max glanced out of the window and saw fearsome faces alongside, contorted with anger, and something heavy and metallic clanged against the fuselage.

Jonathan and Justine were clinging to each other in the seats behind him; if they had noticed Adrienne's absence they were saying nothing. The little plane bumped and juddered, and Max realised they were airborne. He looked down on the group of figures gradually receding beneath them. Eventually they were too small to see clearly any more, and then the plane was surrounded by light, wispy cloud that began to obscure the island from his view.

'What the hell was that all about?!' Bud shouted back from the cockpit.

'Forget it, Bud,' Max called back with weary relief. 'It was nothing.' He became aware that he had been clutching the armrest on the seat so tightly his knuckles had gone white. He relaxed his grip, loosened his seatbelt and turned to face Jonathan and Justine.

'Where's Adrienne?' Jonathan asked.

'She's not coming with us,' Max replied. 'She told me she wanted to stay with Erik, as his slave.'

'What?' Justine gasped. 'Does she know what she's doing?'

Max gazed out of the window, looking vainly for the silhouette of the little island beneath the clouds. He thought of the look that had passed between Erik and Adrienne as he had bade them farewell; a look of pride on his part and loving devotion on hers. 'Oh, yes,' he said, closing his eyes and preparing to sleep, 'she knows exactly what she's doing.'

'I wonder how Adrienne's getting on?' Jonathan asked. 'I'm sure she's fine,' Max replied. 'In fact, I wouldn't be surprised if she was sitting at her husband's feet right now, cuffs round her ankles and a little Erik on the way, and wondering how we're getting on. She did the right thing, you know. She followed her heart, and there aren't many people who are brave enough to do that.'

He turned and smiled at his brother, who was relaxing alongside him in the comfortable sitting room of Max's Suffolk farmhouse. Shot glasses containing finest twelve-year-old Scottish malt whisky stood on the table in front of them, the golden liquid gleaming in the light from the log fire which burned steadily in the fireplace. Outside, the first hard rainfall of autumn pattered against the windows. In a couple of days Jonathan would be returning to St Susan's College, to prepare for the start of term and the new intake of students, but before he went back to Oxford to resume his own teaching, he still had a few lessons of his own to learn.

'I think we should call Justine in, don't you?' Max said idly.

'Is she still sitting in the hall?' Jonathan replied. 'I'd almost forgotten she was there. She'll be so mad. She must have been outside for nearly half an hour, now.'

'Good,' Max said. 'You need to teach Justine the value

204

of patience, Jon. She needs to know that it does get rewarded.'

'Look, if I kept her hanging round after a tutorial for half an hour for no good reason, we'd have such a fight my life wouldn't be worth living.'

'Not any more you won't, I promise you.' Max rose impatiently to his feet. 'Come on, Jon, no second thoughts. This is what she wants. Call her in.'

Jonathan walked over to the door and pulled it open. Justine was sitting on the bottom step of the wide wooden staircase, twisting a strand of her short blonde hair around her index finger.

'Justine, we're ready for you,' Jonathan said.

'And about bloody time, too,' Justine retorted, annoyance clearly audible in her voice. Jonathan wondered how she would react if she knew exactly why she had been kept waiting.

She followed him into the sitting room and stood in the middle of the carpet, hands on her hips, looking at the two brothers. She was dressed in a plain black shift dress that came to mid-thigh and followed the contours of her body, outlining the subtle curves of her breasts and hips. The outfit was completed with sheer black stockings and low-heeled black velvet pumps. This was not the tomboy Justine who had been happy to run round in sweatshirts and jeans; she had acquired a new, womanly poise along with her elegant wardrobe, and it seemed to suit her.

She was wearing a thick silver band around her neck, a present from Jonathan; though it looked like a simple, discreet piece of jewellery perfectly in keeping with the rest of her outfit, both Max and Jonathan knew that it had a deeper significance which would become apparent as the evening progressed.

'Very nice,' Max said, eyeing her up and down. When Max's blue-green eyes met hers, Jonathan noticed that she blushed and lowered her gaze. 'Perfectly dressed for dinner, Justine. It's just a shame we won't be eating for a while.'

'What?' Justine exclaimed. 'But Max, you said dinner would be at half-past six. And it's nearly seven o'clock as it is. Just because the two of you were discussing business it doesn't mean you can forget about eating. Why you have to be so secretive, I just don't know…'

Jonathan winced inwardly. Whatever Justine thought, business had been the last thing on his mind. He and Max had been discussing the possibility of driving over to watch Ipswich take on Portsmouth in the football on Saturday, and the conservatory that Max was planning to build in the garden. There was nothing secretive about it; it was just another of Max's mind games, designed to put Justine in the right frame of mind for what was to follow.

'Just because you're Jon's girlfriend doesn't mean he has to share everything with you,' Max said, watching Justine bristle with indignation at his words.

'Well, whatever the big secret is, can we go and eat now? I'm starving,' Justine complained.

'Justine, I thought your adventures on Odinland would have cured you of this tiresome need for instant gratification, but obviously I was wrong.' Max sighed. 'There are more important things in life than your stomach, and you need to be taught that.'

Jonathan shivered. They were moving into the important part of the proceedings now, and surely Justine must have realised what was coming next. Perhaps she did not know that Max had offered to teach him how to become the dominant master she required, but if that were the case, she would surely not be in doubt for much longer.

'Dinner is going to be delayed for just a little while,' Max said. 'I'm sorry if that inconveniences you, Justine, but you have to understand you're not the only one with priorities.' He sighed, theatrically. 'Though why we're discussing this down here, I don't know. The proper place to deal with your recalcitrance is in the playroom, not the sitting room. But before we go up there, I think you should remove your dress. You won't be needing it, and I'd hate to see it get creased.'

'Max...'

It was only a token protest, Jonathan realised. Justine was aware that she had been set up by the two of them, but the sparkle in her eyes indicated that she was not entirely displeased. He himself was busy taking in every nuance of the exchange between Max and Justine, trying to learn the proper tone and manner to take with his submissive girlfriend. He was excited by the thought of Justine being forced to strip; he was keen to see what she was wearing under the dress, and his cock was beginning to pulse and lengthen slightly in anticipation.

'I'm waiting,' Max said.

Justine reached behind her and unzipped the dress. She pulled it down off her shoulders and let it fall to the carpet, using her hands to conceal her breasts as much as she could while she was doing so for, as was still almost invariably the case, she wore no bra. The tantalising glimpses of her nipples she inadvertently offered to Jonathan showed that they were already beginning to erect, their areolae crinkling at the thought of what was to come. Her underwear consisted of an ivory satin suspender belt, edged with thick lace, holding up her stockings, and a matching pair of lace-fronted knickers, through which the contours of her sex were vaguely visible.

Max said nothing, but smiled in obvious approval. Jonathan hoped she would be told to take off her knickers too, but Max was working to his own agenda, and he walked to the door and held it open.

'Upstairs, please, Justine,' he ordered.

Meekly, with her hands crossed over her breasts, Justine began to walk out of the room. Max shook his head.

'Hands on your head, Justine,' he said.

She did as she was told with only a little hesitation, the movement raising her already uptilted breasts a little higher. Jonathan discreetly adjusted the crotch of his trousers, feeling his erection harden even further.

The three of them made their way upstairs to the playroom, Justine leading the way, Jonathan following her satin-clad bottom with rapt attention and Max bringing up the rear. Justine waited patiently until she was ushered inside; there was no need for Max to lock the door, as there was no chance of an unexpected interruption.

This was the first time Jonathan had been inside the playroom, and he glanced around in wonder, taking in the padded whipping stool, the pillory and the collection of punishment implements hanging from the wall. Until now, he had never realised quite how seriously Max had studied the art of discipline, but everything in this room suggested that his brother really was a master of chastisement, in all senses of the word.

'Next time, I'll let you make the choice of punishment,' Max said to him as Justine stood before the two of them, her flesh goosepimpling with what could only be excitement, for it was not at all cold in this comfortably appointed room. 'For today you can just watch and learn – to begin with at any rate. However, you could help me with the cuffs.'

Max led Justine over to the wall, and together he and Jonathan slipped her wrists into the soft, padded cuffs that hung in readiness on their shining lengths of chain. Closing them securely, the two brothers turned to each other conspiratorially.

'You know you don't have anything to be jealous of,' Max said in a low tone. 'Whatever I do to her today, you'll have the chance to do for the rest of your life.'

Max gazed at Justine, who stood patiently, her hands raised and chained over her head, waiting. Without preamble his hand went straight to her crotch, cupping her quim. He used his middle finger to push the gusset of her satin knickers into the entrance to her sex; as he had expected, she was already a little wet, and the fabric slipped easily inside her.

'Beautiful,' he muttered. 'But they'll have to come off.'

In one swift movement he yanked Justine's knickers down to her knees, and left them there. The soft golden hair had grown back thickly on her mound of Venus since their return to England, and he looked at it with mock distaste. 'I like you better without it,' he said. 'Jonathan, go to my bedroom and fetch my shaving kit.'

Jonathan raced down the hall and into Max's large, airy bedroom. The badger hair shaving brush, mother-of-pearl-handled cutthroat razor and cake of shaving soap were all lying neatly by the marble washbasin in the en suite bathroom. Only Max, thought Jonathan, would use this old-fashioned kit when everyone else had switched to electric shavers or disposable razors. He picked everything up, ran hot water into a mug and grabbed a towel from a heated rail by the washbasin.

Max did not appear to have touched Justine any further

in his absence; he supposed the waiting was as erotic a form of torment as anything else he could devise. Jonathan watched as Max lathered up the brush and spread the creamy foam liberally over Justine's mound and between her legs. He opened the razor and gazed at it. 'I missed using this on Odinland, you know,' he said, pushing Justine's knickers completely off and tossing them to one side. 'Nothing else takes the hair off like it, as little Justine is just about to find out.'

Systematically, he set about removing the hair from Justine's pubic area with long, steady sweeps of the razor. It took only a minute or so before he was patting away the remnants of shaving foam with the soft, white towel, leaving her sex as pink and bare as it had been during her time as Svein's slave. Without it she seemed even more naked, even though she still wore the suspender belt and stockings. All Jonathan wanted to do was fall to his knees and kiss her beautifully vulnerable looking pussy, but he doubted that was what Max was leading up to.

'And now we can begin,' Max said. 'Over the whipping stool, I think.'

Jonathan was a little disappointed; he was enjoying the sight of Justine dangling in the wrist cuffs, but he realised that was not the best position in which to punish her backside. He aided Max in freeing her from the cuffs, and they walked her over to the leather-topped stool and bent her over it.

'Legs apart, please, Justine,' Max ordered, and Justine obediently spread her legs about a foot apart, giving the brothers a perfect view of the furrow between her buttocks and her dark, puckered anal hole. Jonathan smiled, remembering how he had plunged his cock deep into that tight little hole as Justine had lain beneath him on the floor of Svein's hut.

'I've always thought that some women had an arse which was made to be punished,' Max said, running a hand over Justine's firm bottom cheeks. 'Nice and round, plump but not fat, just like this one here. It's just crying out to be soundly whacked.'

He gave Justine's backside an almost absent-minded slap, and she wriggled slightly.

'No, Justine, I want you to stay still. What happens if she doesn't stay still, eh, Jon?'

'Er… we give her a few more slaps?' Jonathan replied.

'Very good. I don't think there's going to be that much I have to teach you. But I want you to watch and learn while I give a small demonstration of a hand spanking.'

He placed his left hand in the small of Justine's back, and raised his right. 'Palm nice and flat, as you can see, Jon, and just apply a little bit of pressure with the other hand to make sure the slave stays in place. We're not going to spank her too hard; I just want to warm up the flesh so you can follow it up with a nice thorough paddling.'

As he spoke, he brought his hand down on Justine's bottom with a sharp report that echoed in the small room. Mindful of her instructions, Justine did not move. Jonathan watched as Max spanked Justine about a dozen times; as he had said, they were not hard blows, and though her skin appeared slightly flushed, she did not look to be finding it too painful.

'Your turn, now,' Max told his brother, and the two exchanged places. Jonathan thought back to the strange, dream-like experience he had undergone in Valhalla, when he had been required to perform a ritual punishment. Then, he had been nervous and unsure. Now, with one hand resting against Justine's soft, warm back, and his other poised to crimson her backside, he felt confident and in control.

His hand fell with a satisfying smacking sound. Justine flinched slightly; the brief pause had seemingly given her nerve-endings enough time to forget that further pain was to be inflicted. Jonathan imitated Max's actions, making scrupulously sure that each slap landed on a different section of skin. The temptation to make Justine squeal and wriggle by increasing the force of his blows was substantial, but Jonathan knew that he had to pace himself. At last Max seemed satisfied with his brother's efforts, and ordered him to stop.

'Take this.' He had taken a thick rubber paddle down from the wall. It reminded Jonathan of a table tennis bat without the dimpled surface, and he smacked it experimentally against his palm.

'It's a good implement for a beginner,' Max explained. 'Later on I'll teach you about canes. They require a little more practice. This is just like your palm, except it never gets tired. Go on, try it.'

Jonathan needed no second invitation. He brought the paddle down on Justine's bottom, hearing the heavy rubber reverberate as it struck her flesh. Quickly getting a feel for the implement, he brought it down again and again. Justine had not been warned how many blows to expect, and after five or six she was beginning to make small noises of discomfort, and jerk her body away in an attempt to avoid the paddle's dull sting. Max had not told Jonathan to stop, so he increased the pressure of his hand in the small of Justine's back, pushing her more firmly against the whipping stool. When he began to use the paddle again, he noticed that Justine was still moving with every blow,

212

but now she was grinding her pubic mound against the black leather, trying to stimulate herself.

Max had noticed this, too, and he ordered Jonathan to stop. 'It seems to me that this slave is taking an obscene amount of pleasure in her punishment, the shameless little slut,' he said. 'Jonathan, how do we ascertain whether the slave is enjoying herself?'

'We check to see if she's wet,' Jonathan replied.

Justine seemed to push her bottom towards him more lewdly as he spoke those words, waiting for the feel of his hand between her legs. She was not disappointed; at a nod from Max, Jonathan ran his index finger between her swollen labia, and brought it away coated with her juices.

'Well, Max, it looks like she's definitely enjoying it.'

'In that case there's only one thing we can do.' As Max spoke, he shrugged out of his jacket and began to unbutton his shirt. Following his lead, Jonathan, too, began to undress. His cock had been growing progressively harder since they had come into the playroom, and it was a relief to free it. As Max pulled down his own boxer shorts, Jonathan noticed that his brother was also erect. Justine, still bending obediently over the whipping stool, could not see any of what was happening, but it must have been obvious to her from the rustling of clothing what the brothers were doing.

Max, naked now, spun Justine round and kissed her hard on the mouth. She responded eagerly, wrapping her arms round the back of his neck and rubbing her body against his. Jonathan felt a pang of envy, but reassured himself with the knowledge that it would soon be his turn.

He watched as Max finally broke the embrace and stepped aside. Justine stepped into Jonathan's embrace, pressing her mouth fiercely against his. The beating seemed to have energised her, and she twined her fingers in his glossy dark hair. He began to bite her lips with little, gentle nips, until they were bruised and swollen with desire.

Max came round to stand behind Justine, his hands caressing her breasts, thumbs and fingers pinching her rosy nipples until they crinkled and she gave a small cry, revelling in the erotic pain. His body was flush with hers, so he could feel the heat emanating from her punished backside.

Jonathan's hands were busy at Justine's crotch now, stroking her smooth, soft mound of Venus and slipping lower to part her dewy labia. He buried a finger deep in her vagina, feeling the inner walls clinging snugly around his knuckle.

'On your knees, little Justine,' Max was whispering in her ear. 'Worship your new master.'

Without hesitation, Justine pulled away from Jonathan's invading finger and dropped to the ground. Her hands closed round the root of his cock, and she held it steady as she formed her mouth into a perfect '0' and encircled the top of his glans. He shuddered as he felt the warm, wet pressure of her lips against his sensitive crown, and almost moaned with sheer dizzy pleasure as the pressure increased and she began to suck in a rhythmical fashion.

Max was urging her to raise her bottom in the air, so he could slide his cock into her soaking pussy. Jonathan could not see the moment of entry, but he felt it, as Justine gasped and his shaft disappeared a little deeper into her mouth. She was skewered between the two brothers, a sturdy penis filling her at both ends, each one demanding to be satisfied.

She set about the task with enthusiasm. Jonathan closed his eyes as her mouth slurped wetly up and down the length of his cock. She took him so deeply into her throat he could feel his pubic hair rasping against her chin. The pace of this fellation was being set by Max, pumping steadily into Justine's sex from behind. He, too, was inside her to the hilt, his balls slapping hard against her reddened arse cheeks as he thrust.

This was heaven, Jonathan thought. It was worth all the torment they had undergone on the island, all the acrimony that had passed between him and Max, to reach this moment when he and his brother were working in perfect harmony to pleasure Justine.

His climax was building in an unstoppable crescendo, and he cried out as jets of his come began to spurt down Justine's throat. Justine's fingers were on her clit, and she was moving towards her own orgasm, a process that was hastened as Max's hips began to spasm convulsively and his thrusts into her body became more frantic. Jonathan could not have said which of the two came first, as Justine collapsed against him and Max clung to her body, sated.

Inevitably, it was Max who recovered first. He glanced over at Jonathan, a thoroughly satisfied smile on his face. 'So, do you think you've learned anything?' he asked his brother.

'I think so,' Jonathan replied with mock hesitation, 'but I'm not entirely sure on some of the finer points. Perhaps we could go through it all just one more time to make sure…?'

On the other side of the Atlantic, Danny Pettersen killed the engine of his boat and stared out into the fog. This would have been a routine coastguard patrol, but for the weird radio messages he had picked up the night before.

The short-wave receiver in his office had crackled into life, and he had heard a voice; like nothing he had known before. And yet, it had triggered a race memory he could not put a name to. It had reminded him, somehow, of his grandfather's voice, cracked and broken with age, singing the songs that *his* grandfather had sung to him, before the family had packed their bags and headed out from Oslo to seek their fortune in the wilds of Newfoundland.

He'd traced the signal out to roughly this area, to the dead island of Odinland. He had heard the stories of the archaeological party who had visited the island in the summer, and seen something among the ruins of that Viking settlement which was so terrible they could not put a name to it. Folks had been saying the island was cursed for longer than he could remember, but he wasn't one for superstitious nonsense. This had been a seductive sound, a sound that called to a place in him the twentieth century had left untouched. It spoke to him of pain, and passion, and pleasure like he had never known. He started the engine again, and headed for whatever might be waiting for him on the shore.

More exciting titles available from Chimera

***

All **Chimera** titles are available from your local bookshop or newsagent, or direct from our mail order department. Please send your order with your credit card details, a cheque or postal order (made payable to *Chimera Publishing Ltd*) to: **Chimera Publishing Ltd., Readers' Services, PO Box 152, Waterlooville, Hants, PO8 9FS**. Or call our **24 hour telephone/fax credit card hotline: +44 (0)23 92 646062** (Visa, Mastercard, Switch, JCB and Solo only).

UK & BFPO - Aimed delivery within three working days.
- A delivery charge of £3.00.
- An item charge of £0.20 per item, up to a maximum of five items.

For example, a customer ordering two items for delivery within the UK will be charged £3.00 delivery + £0.40 items charge, totalling a delivery charge of £3.40. The maximum delivery cost for a UK customer is £4.00. Therefore if you order more than five items for delivery within the UK you will not be charged more than a total of £4.00 for delivery.

Western Europe - Aimed delivery within five to ten working days.
- A delivery charge of £3.00.
- An item charge of £1.25 per item.

For example, a customer ordering two items for delivery to W. Europe, will be charged £3.00 delivery + £2.50 items charge, totalling a delivery charge of £5.50.

USA - Aimed delivery within twelve to fifteen working days.
- A delivery charge of £3.00.
- An item charge of £2.00 per item.

For example, a customer ordering two items for delivery to the USA, will be charged £3.00 delivery + £4.00 item charge, totalling a delivery charge of £7.00.

Rest of the World - Aimed delivery within fifteen to twenty-two working days.
- A delivery charge of £3.00.
- An item charge of £2.75 per item.

For example, a customer ordering two items for delivery to the ROW, will be charged £3.00 delivery + £5.50 item charge, totalling a delivery charge of £8.50.

For a copy of our free catalogue please write to

Chimera Publishing Ltd
Readers' Services
PO Box 152
Waterlooville
Hants
PO8 9FS

or e-mail us at
info@chimerabooks.co.uk

or purchase from our range of superbly erotic titles at
www.chimerabooks.co.uk

*Titles £5.99. **£7.99. **All others £6.99**

The full range of our wonderfully erotic titles are also
available as downloadable e-books at our website

www.chimerabooks.co.uk

Chimera Publishing Ltd

PO Box 152
Waterlooville
Hants
PO8 9FS

www.chimerabooks.co.uk

info@chimerabooks.co.uk

www.chimeradating.co.uk

***

Sales and Distribution in the USA and Canada

Client Distribution Services, Inc
193 Edwards Drive
Jackson
TN 38301
USA

***

Sales and Distribution in Australia

Dennis Jones & Associates Pty Ltd
19a Michellan Ct
Bayswater
Victoria
Australia 3153